sisters of the heart

best buddies

soul sister

friends forever

kindred spirits

sister-friends

SISTERCHICKS
Down Under!

girlfriends

pals for life

chum

confidante

gal pals

true blue

ally

"I just finished *Sisterchicks do the Hula!* and I loved it! Actually, I found myself sneaking into the bathroom away from my loving husband and ever-present children to read more. You have written marvelous fiction that leaves me feeling closer to God."—MARY

"A coworker has me hooked on your books, and they are fabulous! A bunch of us at work decided that we're Sisterchicks, and we can't wait for the next adventure, because we're all going to read the book simultaneously and discuss it at lunch. Thanks for making work a fun place to be all of a sudden!" —LAUREN

"I am from the UK. Last weekend I bought *Sisterchicks on the Loose!* I can honestly say I never in my life read a book so fast! I laughed out loud, even cried in places, and struggled to put it down. It made me realise I, too, have a Sisterchick who should be treasured."—TRACEY

"A friend gave *Sisterchicks do the Hula!* to me for my birthday. I couldn't put it down. I'm thirty-five and feeling way too old for my age. Thank you for the breath of fresh air. I felt like God had you write it just for me!—KARA

"I just finished *Sisterchicks on the Loose!* and loved it. In fact, I devoured it. I hated to see it end. It had to be one of the best books on friendship that I have read. Love your sense of humor; I laughed out loud many times reading it. You have such a heart for Jesus and a wonderful spirit."—DEBBIE

"Thank you for the return trip to Oahu this morning! *[Sisterchicks do the Hula!]* It is snowing and sleeting outside, but I was enjoying the beautiful blues that only Hawai'i has. Thank you for giving me a 'garland of hosannas' and for reminding me to do the hula with God's rhythm of grace." —MARBARA

a sisterchick™ novel

SISTERCHICKS
Down Under!

ROBIN JONES GUNN

Multnomah® Publishers *Sisters, Oregon*

SISTERCHICKS DOWN UNDER!
published by Multnomah Publishers, Inc.

© 2005 by Robin's Ink, LLC
International Standard Book Number: 1-59052-411-X

Sisterchicks is a trademark of Multnomah Publishers, Inc.

Cover image of women by Bill Cannon Photography, Inc.
Painting referenced on p. 161 is entitled *The Sea Hath Its Pearls*
by William Henry Margetson

Scripture quotations are from:
The Message
© 1993, 1994, 1995, 1996, 2000, 2001, 2002
Used by permission of NavPress Publishing Group
The Holy Bible, New King James Version © 1984 by Thomas Nelson, Inc.
Holy Bible, New Living Translation © 1996
Used by permission of Tyndale House Publishers, Inc.
All rights reserved.
HOLY BIBLE: EASY-TO-READ VERSION
© 2001 by World Bible Translation Center, Inc. and used by permission.

Multnomah is a trademark of Multnomah Publishers, Inc.
and is registered in the U.S. Patent and Trademark Office.
The colophon is a trademark of Multnomah Publishers, Inc.

Printed in the United States of America

For information:
MULTNOMAH PUBLISHERS, INC. • P.O. BOX 1720 • SISTERS, OR 97759

Library of Congress Cataloging-in-Publication Data

Gunn, Robin Jones, 1955-
 Sisterchicks down under! : a Sisterchicks novel / Robin Jones Gunn.
     p. cm.
 ISBN 1-59052-411-X
     1. Canadians—Australia—Fiction.   2. Women   travelers—Fiction.
 3. Australia—Fiction. 4. Sisters—Fiction. I. Title.
     PS3557.U4866S5625 2005
     813'.54—dc22

                              2004029514

        05 06 07 08 09 10—10 9 8 7 6 5 4 3 2 1 0

Acknowledgments

With a grateful g'day to the wonderful people who contributed
to this story:

Ross, my one true love.

Bill, my visioneer.

Don, Doug, Brian, and Kevin, who sent me down under in
search of a good story.

Bruce and Paul, who met me in Sydney and gave me a bag
of Cheerios to feed the kangaroos.

Mike, Noel, and Ted, who showed me the best of their
beloved New Zealand.

Susanne, you are a gifted hostess. Thank you for opening
your heart and home to me. Loved your Pavlova!

Frances, thank you for taking me to corners of New
Zealand that will never leave my heart.

Carol, Joanne, Penny, Robin, Tania, and Tracey, you amazing women proved my theory to be correct: Sisterchicks are
everywhere!

Mostly what God does is love you.
Keep company with him and learn a life of love.
Observe how Christ loved us.
His love was not cautious but extravagant.
He didn't love in order to get something from us
but to give everything of himself to us.
Love like that.

EPHESIANS 5:2

Prologue

Age is just a number, right?

That's what I thought until three years ago when my younger brother opened his big mouth. He was on his way to Mexico to settle the legal details on some property his wife had inherited when he stopped by our home in southern California. His life seemed brimming with new adventures, while Tony and I were riding the overly-committed-to-the-schedule freight train we had been on since we got married.

Over dinner my brother joked about his receding hairline. "You know, Kathleen, you're halfway there yourself."

"No I'm not." I pulled at the strands of my straight brown hair to prove that my dependable mane wasn't falling out.

"I meant your age," he said. "You turned forty-five last month, right? You could be halfway done." He seemed to wait for me to do the math.

I always hated math.

I felt as if an equation had etched itself on the chalkboard of my mind: $45 + x = ?$

I didn't know the answer.

What had my forty-five years added up to so far? What was the value of x that would fill the remaining years? What would the sum of my life be? And what risks was I willing to take to solve the equation?

Apparently God can use all things—including math—to prepare a hurried heart to respond to Him when He's about to do a new thing. If I hadn't been pondering the "value of x" for so many weeks after my brother's visit, I don't think I would have been ready for what followed.

In the middle of the night, Tony's old boss, Mad Dog, called from Wellington, New Zealand, to offer Tony a three-month position film editing at Jackamond Studios. Ever since the success of *The Lord of the Rings*, Wellington had become *the* location for up-and-coming filmmakers. Tony saw the job as the big break he had been waiting for. I saw it as an opportunity to step off the edge of my well-padded nest and take a free fall into the unknown.

After all, our daughter was in college, and we were no longer financially responsible for my mother-in-law's convalescent care. Tony and I could do this. We could leave everything for three months and have the exotic travel experience we had only dreamed about during our college days.

I always do my best thinking while shaving my legs in a tubful of bubbles. The two weeks prior to our departure for Wellington, I had the smoothest legs and the most wrinkled fingers in all of Los Angeles.

I'd thought through every detail and confidently arrived at the airport with everything I needed. Everything, that is, except one item I hadn't tucked in my suitcases or sent ahead in the boxes. I didn't pack a single friend. After spending most of my life in the same city, same church, and same circles, I suddenly was minus my built-in community of friends.

Looking back, I now see how unnatural it was to change a well-established migratory route in the middle of life and expect my wings to start flapping in rhythm as soon as I took the free fall. It shouldn't have been such a surprise that I fell so hard. After all, everything in my world had flip-flopped.

I think it was necessary, though, for me to tumble as far down under as I did. Otherwise, I never would have stumbled into the Chocolate Fish on a fine fall Friday in February with feathers in my hair. And that's where I found Jill.

If Jill were the one telling this story, she would say that's where she found *me*. But I'm saying that's where I found her. It had become clear that to solve the math problem written over this season of my life, I needed one more whole number. That little number was one. One new best friend. Jill.

Jill likes math. She sees math in art and nature and isn't afraid of the unknown equations. Two years ago when she and I stood in front of a painting at an Australian art museum in Sydney, she opened my eyes to the beauty of balance and symmetry, and that's when I began to make peace with math.

But before I flutter through our story, I will add one more important point. I believe the reason I found Jill wasn't so much because I was looking for her, but because she was waiting for me, hanging by her painted toenails on the edge of her own empty nest.

One

During the two weeks before we left for New Zealand, every day felt like a storm at sea. My husband turned into a ruthless commander, as the intensity of it all swept us through our final days in California. When the storm subsided, I found myself washed up at an unfamiliar airport on the underside of the globe.

The only comforting sight was the grinning face of Tony's boss, Marcus, aka "Mad Dog," who met us at the baggage claim in Wellington. He punched Tony in the arm. "What did you think of that flight? Was I right about its being a marathon film fest? How many did you watch?"

"Five. No seven. No, I think it was five." Tony's adrenaline-induced gaze seemed frozen on his face.

Mad Dog adjusted his frayed corduroy cap. "Do you want to eat something first or go right to your new place?"

"Home," I said, as if it were a secret password that would lead me into this new world. All I needed was my new space around me so I could start fluffing up things the way I liked.

Then I would be ready to remind myself why this had been a good decision.

"Home it is. Hope you guys like this place. I told you how hard it is to find housing near the studio, didn't I?"

"You did," Tony said. "And we really appreciate all you did to find us a place. I'm going to owe you big time."

"You can pay me back with a few hours of overtime." Mad Dog loaded our luggage into the back of a van he had borrowed from Walter Jackamond Studios.

"How many hours are a 'few,' Marcus?" I asked.

He let out a single gut sound that resembled a cross between a cough and a guffaw. In the twelve years we had known him, I still hadn't gotten used to his laugh.

"You have to start calling me Mad Dog," he said. "No one here knows me as Marcus. And when I say a few hours, I mean…"

He didn't finish his sentence, but I realized I already knew the answer. For the next three months, Jackamond Studios would occupy my husband's every waking hour. Not only because they were behind schedule on the project for which they had hired Tony, but also because my husband never did anything halfway.

"Hey, it's Gollum!" Tony pointed to the roof of the terminal. An enormous model of the bald, grim-faced Middle-earth icon peered down on us, looking like a gigantic alien that had fallen to earth and gotten his foot stuck through the roof.

"I guess we're not in Kansas anymore, Toto," I said.

Tony gave me a gratuitous wink at my attempt to make a joke. I gripped the car door's handle. Not because of Tony's wink or Gollum's glare, but because Mad Dog was driving on the left side of the road.

Tony laughed. "This is wild!"

"You'll get used to it," Mad Dog said. "Only took me a week when I moved here. Maybe less."

I expected an oncoming car to ram into us any moment. Everyone was going the opposite from what my brain said was correct. Mad Dog drove past a row of low-rise buildings, and I tried to take it all in. Stop lights, a normal-looking city bus, lots of small cars, billboards—and all of a sudden an Esprit store. All the evidences of Western civilization were here; yet it felt so different.

"There's the Embassy," Mad Dog said with reverence. He pointed to a pale yellow vintage square building. Fixed on the roof was another creature born in Tolkien's imagination. This one looked like a swooping black dragon with a long neck.

"How strange that the U.S. Embassy would have a dragon movie prop on top of it," I said.

Mad Dog and Tony both looked at me as if I were an alien creature who had just stuck my foot through the roof and landed in the same car with them.

"What?"

"Kathleen," Tony said patiently, "that's not the U.S. Embassy. That's the Embassy Theatre. And on the roof that's a fell beast ridden by a Ringwraith."

I kept a fixed expression and didn't blink, waiting for Tony to give me a few more hints as to why that should ring any bells.

"Remember the photos we saw of the premier? Opening night?"

"They still had Gollum on the roof of the Embassy for the premier," Mad Dog said. "Maybe that's why you didn't recognize it."

"Oh, yeah. I'm sure that's the reason." I diverted my gaze out the window. I hoped I wouldn't be tested on any more *Lord of the Rings* trivia before we completed the last few miles of a very long journey to our new home.

We turned onto a narrow road and followed a pristine bay that skirted Wellington like a fancy azure petticoat. Thousands of houses dotted the low, rolling green hills that rose from the bay.

I noticed that some of the trees were beginning to drop their leaves. Autumn was coming to the globe's underside. At home I had left budding jacaranda trees. My going away party at work had been decorated with fresh tulips and spring daffodils. Here, the leaves were turning gold.

I was in a flip-flopped place, inside and out.

Mad Dog slowed the van as we entered a residential area. "See that house over there?" He pointed at a tidy bungalow that was about eight hundred square feet big.

"That place just sold for the equivalent of two hundred and fifty thousand dollars. U.S. dollars. Not New Zealand dollars. Like I said, it was amazing I found a place near the studio for the exact rent you said you wanted to pay. And it comes with a refrigerator."

I should have known when he listed the refrigerator as a plus that I should brace myself.

"If you don't take it, another guy at work wants it."

"I'm sure we'll want it," I said.

Tony voiced his agreement.

Mad Dog stopped the car. "This is it. What do you think?"

I peered out the car window at another bungalow-style house. The first thing I noticed was the grinning figurine standing his post in front of a narrow row of yellow and orange mums. I'd seen a number of lawn gnomes in my day and a pink flamingo or two, but this was the first ceramic hobbit I'd ever seen guarding a flower bed.

"Cute," I said with a smile. "But the hobbit definitely needs to go."

Mad Dog let out his guffaw laugh. "You'll have to clear that one with Mr. Barry, the landlord. What do you think of the garage?"

The tiny building that was separate from the main house had a window in front with curtains. It reminded me of the toolshed my father had built in our backyard when I was a girl. My two sisters and I wanted to turn the shed into a playhouse, but Dad never let us.

"The garage is cute, too." I turned my attention to the main house. The bungalow appeared to be freshly painted in a soft shade of celery green with white trim around the two front windows. It was much smaller than our home in Tustin, but I could make this cottage into "our" place for three months.

"You think this will work for you?" Mad Dog asked.

"Yes." I nodded and looked to see if Tony agreed. He did.

"You got a good woman, Tony." Mad Dog reached into the back of the van for our luggage. "Last week a guy who came down here from Canoga Park left after ten days on the job. His wife said she couldn't live in such primitive conditions. She said he had to decide between her or the job. He picked her."

"Good choice." I looped a shoulder bag over my arm and reached for another bag.

Mad Dog looked at me with his eyebrows raised. "If you say so."

I headed for the front door and was at the doorstep when

Mad Dog called, "Kathleen, over here." He was standing by the garage's side door.

I stumbled through the grass and past the lantern-holding, smirking hobbit and wondered if the house key was hidden in the garage. Or maybe Mad Dog wanted to give us the full tour before we went inside the house.

He opened the garage's side door. Tony stepped in first. I followed, and the lights turned on. Literally.

This was it. We were "home."

Barely breathing, I dropped both the shoulder bags and stood in the middle of our garage apartment. The single room came with a bed covered in an overly bright floral bedspread, a corner table, two metal patio chairs, a sink, an armchair, a hot plate, and the prized feature—a dorm-sized refrigerator.

"Bathroom is back there." Mad Dog pointed to a door that looked as if it should open to the backyard.

I looked at Tony. He wasn't moving. Or blinking.

With quiet steps, I wove my way through the furniture to the closed door and opened it. The newly built bathroom/laundry room/storage room/closet space was nearly half the size of the entire garage apartment. The room had been beautifully finished and was by far the nicest part of the apartment. The white curtains fluttered as a cool breeze came through the open window and coaxed me to breathe again.

I looked at the bathtub, my usual place of retreat and reflection in times of stress. The inner sanctum was defiled by a wooden drying rack propped up inside it. Over the rack was draped a pair of men's briefs. Not just any briefs, but giant-sized briefs.

The cry of distress that had been welling up inside me came out in two unexpected words. "Jumbo briefs!"

"What?" Tony came over to me.

I pointed and blinked so I wouldn't cry.

"Who would've left their underwear in here?" Tony asked.

"They look a little too large to belong to the garden hobbit," I said in a pathetically squeaky voice.

Mad Dog cracked up, his cough-laugh bouncing off the walls. "You keep that sense of humor going, Kathleen, and you'll be fine."

I pressed my lips together and felt my heart swell with empathy for the wife from Canoga Park. Perhaps she had been the tenant in this toolshed before us. Her departure might have been the reason Mad Dog was able to find a place for us. Perhaps the jumbo briefs were her husband's and had been left in their hasty departure.

"You paid the first month's rent already, right?" Tony asked.

Mad Dog nodded. "I had to grab the place as soon as it opened up, since nothing else is for rent in this neighborhood. You'd have more options if you decided to buy a car."

Tony glanced my way. Our discussions about simplifying life during these three months had sounded so noble and appealing when we were in California working out a plan. We agreed that we needed to do this without the expense of a car. Obviously both of us thought the amount we had set aside for rent would have resulted in a lot more living space than it had.

"What can I do to help you guys settle in?" Mad Dog asked. I recognized in his voice a commendable effort to put a positive spin on the situation.

"We can take it from here." Tony stepped into the other room and checked out the premium unused space under the bed.

"You'll need some groceries." Mad Dog apparently wasn't

willing to leave so quickly. "I can drive you to the store, unless you want to walk down to the dairy. That's what they call the corner market around here. Or, hey, I know a great place for fish and chips. You have to eat fish and chips your first day here. We could all drive there now."

Tony looked at me, and I returned his numb gaze. I wasn't ready to sit with another seat belt around me for any reason. Even if food was waiting at the end of the journey.

"Do you want to stay here, Kath? I'll take a run with Mad Dog to get some food." Tony opened the refrigerator, as if sizing up how much space he had to fill. His mind was always editing, arranging, and adjusting to fit the parameters of a given situation.

Once Mad Dog left, I would let Tony know that too much information had been edited from our housing arrangements. This place was not going to be okay. Not for ninety days and ninety nights. Not when Tony was the one who would be going to work every day, and I would be the one sitting here with nothing to do.

We don't have to stay here. We can find another place. This is just for a night or two. We won't even need to unpack. This is very temporary.

"Anything you want me to bring back for you, Kathleen?"

I mouthed the word *chocolate*.

My knowing husband nodded. "Anything else?"

"After the chocolate it doesn't matter."

Tony and Mad Dog opened the door to leave, and there stood our landlord with his large fist raised, as if he were about to knock. He was huge. Gigantic enough to fit into the briefs occupying the hallowed bathtub space.

In a deep voice with a New Zealand accent, Mr. Barry

boomed out his greeting. Then he ducked the way I remembered Gandalf ducking to enter Bilbo Baggins's house in the Shire. Mr. Barry seemed to fill the room. Suddenly the joke seemed to be on me. I was the hobbit!

I tried to keep my jet-lagged self from bursting into laughter. Not a friendly chuckle sort of laugh. Welling up inside me was the sort of unladylike, explosive laugh that accompanies any truly successful preteen girls' sleepover.

I couldn't hold it in. The laughter spilled out. I couldn't help it. I'd never before met a giant's underwear before I met him.

"Jet lag," Tony said graciously.

I composed myself, and Mr. Barry told us all the important specifics of the apartment, including trash pickup and making the next rent payment. I only half listened, confident we wouldn't be here by the time the trash was ready for pickup.

As soon as all the guys left, I flopped onto the surprisingly comfortable bed. My head was pounding.

How many days do we have before Tony starts work? Three? No, wait. What day is this?

We flew out of LAX on Tuesday night. We lost a day when we crossed the international date line, so that made today Thursday. At least I thought it was Thursday.

I am so lost. What are we doing here?

I promised myself that regardless of what day it was, before Monday arrived, Tony and I would be settled in a real nest. All I had to do right now was float a little longer.

Tony and Mad Dog returned with a bundle of newspapers that Tony placed on our tiny table. He pulled back the pages. In the center were half a dozen large pieces of breaded, deep-fried fish and a mound of French fries. The excess oil from the fish and chips had soaked through the thin paper on which the fish were separated from the layers of daily news. I found the odor of the oil on the dried newspaper ink inviting.

"Here's the malt vinegar." Mad Dog pulled several small plastic packets from his back pocket. "You have to try it with the vinegar."

I sat in the armchair and enjoyed the fish and chips while Tony unpacked the groceries.

"I'm not sure where we're going to put all this food," he said.

"I told your man he was buying too much," Mad Dog said.

"Tony, all we needed was some snacks, milk, and Cheerios to get us through breakfast tomorrow."

"Did you say *Cheerios*?" Tony held up a package of what looked like little red-skinned sausages. "This is what they call *cheerios* around here."

"No cereal Cheerios?"

Tony shook his head.

"Oh."

Three months without my favorite breakfast food felt almost as shocking as the first sight of this garage apartment. It was all I could do to keep from crying. Over cereal. Or maybe it really was the jet lag. My throat hurt, and one of my ears hadn't popped yet. I just wanted to go home.

Mad Dog left after the fish and chips were devoured. Tony leaned against the closed door and looked around. "Well, what do you think?"

I told Tony every single thought down to my opinion of the obnoxiously bright floral bedspread that dominated the room.

Tony selected that problem as the first he would attempt to solve. "You think it's too bright? Really?"

I was fired up and let my words fly. "It's so blazingly bright that I feel like we could gather around and roast hot dogs in the visual heat it gives off."

"Or roast cheerios." Tony grinned.

"That's not funny." I clenched my jaw.

"Kathleen, relax! It's just the name of a breakfast cereal."

"Apparently it's not! Not in this country, at least!"

Tony laughed at my fury, and that was his mistake.

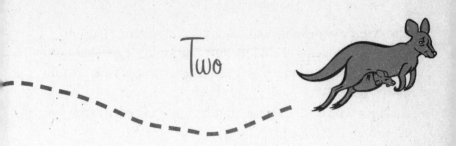

Two

To retell all the things that were said and done during our first two weeks in that toolshed apartment would have no redeeming value. I will simply confess that the worst in me met the worst in Tony, and I don't ever want to go through an experience like that again.

The conclusion was that we weren't able to find alternate housing. We didn't buy a car. Tony "stopped by" the studio within five hours of our arrival in Wellington, and I became a studio widow much sooner than I'd expected.

My survival therapy included many long, hot baths; every variety of Cadbury chocolate available at the corner dairy; a stack of magazines; and a lot of sleep in our comfortable bed with the bedspread turned to the plain side. I refused to eat any cheerio sausages, and I cried every day.

At the end of the second week of my extravagant self-pity, Tony came home on a bicycle. My project-energized husband had stayed his course during that horrible first two weeks with a fresh sense of definition and fortitude. I had been legitimately ill with a terrible head cold the first four or five days after our arrival and slept as much as I could. After I was better, I still wasn't "better."

"I got a bike." Tony wheeled it into the only open space by the sink and refrigerator.

"So I see."

"One of the guys gave it to me, because he bought a new one over the weekend. I thought you and I could buy another one and go for rides together."

I had no words to express to Tony what a bad idea that was. A bicycle wouldn't "fix" what I had. I hadn't ridden a bike since I was a kid. Why would I want to start again now?

"Did you go out this morning?" He motioned toward the stack of magazines beside me. I was still in my pj's, nestled under the covers, but Tony knew the only way I could get more magazines was by walking to the dairy.

"No, I already had these," I said defensively.

He came closer, scrutinizing the headlines and pictures on the covers. "What possible value do you gain from reading this sort of stuff?"

What Tony didn't realize was that he was talking disrespectfully of my friends. And in front of them, no less. The people in these magazines had been my only companions since we had arrived.

"Hey, do I start criticizing the way you spend your day the minute you walk in here?"

Tony raised his eyebrows but quickly edited his usual comeback. We'd already had this argument. A couple of times. He spent his days profitably, immersed in his dream job. Me? I had no reason to get up in the morning. In seventy-four days we would leave here, and I'd get back my life. But for now, the only option I could see was hibernation.

Tony positioned himself rigidly against the counter and lowered his voice. "Kathleen, listen."

I steadied myself for the worst. Whenever he edited his thoughts to a two-word sentence, and my full name was one of the two words, I knew it wouldn't be good.

"What do you need?" he asked.

"Not a bike."

"What then?"

"I don't know."

He seemed to be working very hard to get the next sentence to come out of his mouth. When it did, I knew he meant it.

"Do you want us to go back home?"

My first thought was, *Yes!* Then some long-buried competitive seed inside me sprouted, and I thought of how I'd barely lasted longer than the woman from Canoga Park. I could do better than that. Much better.

I stared at Tony but didn't give him any feedback with my words or my expression. This man, who was looking at me with sincere tenderness, had sold his father's rare coin collection to buy my engagement ring. He had been there for me every moment during our two miscarriages. In our wedding vows, I had drawn from the book of Ruth and promised, "Where you go, I will go; where you live, I will live. Your people will be my people, your God will be my God."

And now he was willing to give up his dream job to restore my sanity.

I hated what I had become. Instead of an adventurous

mama bird on a three-month sabbatical from work and routine who soared through new experiences, I'd tucked my head under my wing and folded up inside myself.

Blinking away a tear, I looked down at the magazine beside me. Details of a celebrity's messy divorce were splashed across the front.

"No." I shook my head and met Tony's gaze. "I don't want to leave. We need to stay here."

"Are you sure?"

I nodded, and with a firm voice I said, "Yes, I'm sure."

Tony looked as if he were trying to mask his relief and select his next words carefully. "Okay. Then if we're going to stay, and we both agree about that, what do you need to make this time in New Zealand work for you? You have to tell me what you need."

I paused. Not a single thought came to mind. Whenever my friend Patsy went on autopilot like this at work, she would say, "This is why they put the word *pause* in *menopause*." Were more changes happening inside me than I realized?

"I honestly don't know," I said at last. My voice was more tender than it had been in two weeks. "I don't know what I need."

"What about doing some travel while we're here? Mad Dog went to Christchurch a few months ago. It's on the South Island. He said it reminded him of Oxford, in England. You always wanted to go to England. You could go with a tour group or something. There's a lot more to New Zealand than Wellywood."

"Than what?"

"Wellywood. That's what employees at the studio call Wellington because it's a little Hollywood."

I realized Tony was even picking up lingo from the locals. The only local I'd talked to besides Mr. Barry was Mrs. Patel at the corner dairy, and she was from India.

"Look, Kath, this is how I see it." Tony reached for my hand. "It doesn't matter to me if you go on a tour. My point is that, for as long as I can remember, you've poured out yourself and your time for everyone else. I've felt bad that you've had to work for us to get by financially. You know that."

"I wanted to work. Besides, we live in an expensive part of the country."

"I know, but I thought that coming here would be a good thing for you, too. It wasn't supposed to just be for me. I never thought this experience would empty you. It was meant to fill you."

All the anger in my heart dissolved. I told Tony I wanted to be there for him the way he had always been there for me. He told me our marriage was more important than any job in any corner of this green earth. I knew he meant it. I also knew I could do a whole lot better at adjusting than I had. I hadn't even tried.

The next morning, with the warmth of my best kiss on his lips, Tony boarded his shiny new bike and took off for work, whistling like the happiest man in the world.

I took a shower, dressed, made the bed, opened the windows, and thoroughly cleaned our neglected living space. Then I took on the challenge of washing our garments from the previously untouched mound of dirty clothes. The garage laundry room didn't come with a dryer; so I filled a basket with the wet items and headed for the backyard.

It was nearly noon and a beautiful, sunny day with a softness in the air. I made my way to the umbrella clothesline in the unfenced yard and pinned up our clean clothes. The say-ing, "airing your laundry," took on new meaning as I realized that, when you hang your clothes out to dry, you really do have fewer secrets from your neighbors.

"Wondered when we'd be seeing you." Mr. Barry's deep voice startled me.

I spun around. "Hello, Mr. Barry. How are you?"

"No complaints."

"Is it okay with you if I use the clothesline today?"

"I don't mind, if you don't mind."

"I was wondering, Mr. Barry. Is there a place nearby where I can get a coffee?"

I hadn't had what I considered a decent cup of coffee since we'd arrived. I didn't want to sound like a whiny American who was going through separation anxiety from her favorite barista, even if that was the truth.

"The Chocolate Fish is down the road by the sandy cove." He pointed me in the right direction. "Go right and follow the street around the curve for about a kilometer. You can't miss it."

"Thanks." I gave a friendly wave and went back inside for my wallet. If I was making a fresh start of it, nothing would help more than a grande mocha latte and a walk on the beach.

I was about a block away from the apartment when I heard a bird singing an unfamiliar twitter in the tree across the road. I was used to the doves' low cooing in two orange trees that sepa-rated our ranch-style home in Tustin from our neighbors'. The fragrance of the spring orange blossoms was just beginning to lace the air when I left home. I didn't recognize the scent in the Wellington air. The breeze had an Indian summer calm and warmth to it, but the scent in the air was sweet. Jasmine maybe? Honeysuckle?

Trotting past more cottage-sized houses, I rounded a bend and noted that larger, more elaborate homes were built on an imposing hill on the left side of the road.

Two more feathered friends overhead twittered the birdsong I didn't recognize. I stopped under the tree, peering up through the stained glass–looking leaves, trying to see what kind of bird was making that sound. A flurry of leaf rustling produced no birds, but a few leaves and feathers came raining down on me. I closed my eyes and waited for a leaf to touch my face. In southern California the seasonal changes were subtle. I was trying my best to enter into the New Zealand autumn.

Continuing on, I came upon the cove Mr. Barry had mentioned. Large granite formations jutted out of the water, providing solitary islands for the seagulls. Far across the blue-green water rose the neighboring hills of this irregular-shaped inlet. I stopped to look over the small, sandy beach. No one was in view.

Slipping off my shoes, I wedged my bare feet into the cold sand and quietly made my peace with God. I knew He never wasted any life experience. He had dreams for me even here in New Zealand. I believed that. But since we arrived, I hadn't asked Him what His dreams were for me. I'd only asked over and over what I was doing here. The answer to what I was "doing" in New Zealand so far had been obvious—nothing. But that was about to change. My heart was tender now. I was ready.

Across the narrow road from the turnout where I'd taken the steps down to the beach, I noticed a funky, elongated green building. The small sign in front told me this was the café Mr. Barry had mentioned.

Eager to sit on the covered front patio and sip a mocha latte, I dusted off my sandy feet and headed across the street. I entered the café and immediately was taken in with the charm and simplicity of the eclectic atmosphere. All the tables along the front windows were occupied except one. I went to that table and pulled out a brightly painted chair that bore the words: "Caution. Seagulls." The chair across the table bore a single red stripe and the neatly printed word: "Wellington."

Trying not to be obvious, I glanced at the woman sitting at the table across from me. She had beautiful, sun-kissed, tawny hair that fell smoothly to her shoulders. Her face was turned toward the window where her gaze stayed fixed on the endless sea. Translucent tears rolled down her cheeks while she did nothing to stop them, blot them, or in any other way acknowledge them. The tears seemed somehow fitting, as if this was her place to be right now, and the reason she was here was to shed tears.

All around us hummed the sounds of clattering plates, water running in a sink, and the buzz of half a dozen conversations spiked with a few dots of laughter. She didn't seem to notice any of it.

I spotted a message on the chalkboard that invited me to place my order at the counter. Beside the counter was a glass pastry case filled with sweets and rolls. Taking my place in line, I waited for the woman in front of me who had a toddler balanced on her hip. His New Zealand accent sounded adorable as he asked his "mummy" if he could have a "fluffy."

"Yes, Jordan. I ordered a fluffy for you and Logan. Now here's a chocolate fish for each of you."

"Yummy!" He took two candies from the woman at the register. The long, fish-shaped treats were covered with chocolate, and the first one immediately went into his mouth.

I smiled at the cute tyke and stepped forward to order. "I'd like one of those candies and a mocha latte."

"And just what have you done today?" the young woman asked in a friendly yet clipped manner. She seemed to be staring at the top of my head.

"Excuse me?"

"For the chocolate fish. What have you done to warrant a sweetie?"

I lowered my voice and tried to subdue my American accent, as I explained that I didn't understand what she was asking.

"Have you never heard that saying? You do something well, and someone says, 'Well done. Here's your chocolate fish.'"

"No, I guess that's one of many new expressions for me."

She tilted her head, and I thought she was trying to decide if she believed me or if I was making fun of what was apparently a well-known New Zealand saying. It turned out to be neither when she asked again, "So, what was your great accomplishment today?"

I felt heat race up my neck as my embarrassment rose. It was either that, or I was having my first hot flash.

This young woman had no idea what an accomplishment it had been for me to get out of bed and get myself here. But I knew. With my chin raised I declared, "I got up this morning."

She seemed to think I was making a clever joke. "Good for you. Have a chocolate fish. We'll bring your mocha to the table."

She handed me the soft, chewy treat. It was about four inches long and about as thick as a fluffy flapjack. The center was pink. It tasted like I was eating a chocolate-covered marshmallow. The burst of sweetness made me smile.

The woman with the beautiful, honey golden hair looked up at me as I slipped past her table. Our eyes met, and she offered me a half smile. A few tears still glistened on her fair skin. She, too, looked up at the top of my head.

Popping the last bit of the chocolate fish into my mouth, I cautiously moved my hand to the back of my head to see if my hair was sticking up. I discovered two white-tipped feathers caught in my hair. Then I remembered the trees I'd passed under and how I'd stopped to close my eyes and listen to the chittering birds.

"A little souvenir," I said with a shrug and a nervous laugh. "From my walk over here."

I tucked the feathers into the pocket of my jeans and headed for my waiting chair, but she stopped me.

"You're an American!" the woman said, her Yankee accent echoing mine.

"Yes." I swallowed the last of my fish and checked my lips for any stray bits of chocolate.

"Have you lived here long?"

"Just two weeks. My husband is working on a project at Jackamond Studios."

"Really?" She looked as if that bit of information struck a chord.

"What about you? Do you live here?"

"Yes." She paused before adding, "We moved here six years ago. Just like you, we came because my husband was offered a job at Jackamond."

"Really! I'm Kathleen, by the way. Kathleen Salerno."

"Jill Radovich." She motioned to the vacant chair across from her. "Would you like to join me? Or are you waiting for someone?"

"No, I'm all alone." Even though I'd been telling myself the same thing for a week, suddenly the hopelessness I'd attached to that phrase was gone. Being alone also meant being open and available for whatever possibilities might come my way.

"Did you by any chance come from California?" Jill asked.

"Yes, southern California."

"What part?"

"Orange County."

She leaned forward, and I noticed all her tears were gone. "What part of Orange County?"

"Tustin."

"What street?" Her smile told me she had heard of Tustin.

"Schilling. It's off of Seventeenth and…"

Jill nodded, her expression brightening. "I know exactly where Schilling is. My maiden name is Schilling. Your street is named after my grandfather. He owned all the Schilling Orange Groves."

"You're kidding!"

"No. I grew up in Tustin. Do you know where the two-story Victorian house is with the wraparound front porch? It was turned into a restaurant."

"Yes, the Fontaine Restaurant."

"My grandfather built that house. We lived there until I graduated from Foothill High School."

"You went to Foothill? So did I!"

We compared the years we were at Foothill and found that Jill had graduated four years ahead of me.

"We were almost there at the same time!" Jill said.

"This is unbelievable! My husband, Tony, and I have a house less than three blocks from the Fontaine Restaurant. As a matter of fact, we have two huge orange trees in our side yard.

They were there when we moved in. I'm sure they were planted by your grandfather."

Jill pressed her lips together, and for a moment neither of us spoke.

She drew in a steady breath. "I remember the day the bulldozers started uprooting the trees to clear the grove."

"That must have been awful for your family, seeing all those trees go."

She nodded. "Some of the trees were diseased and needed to be taken out. Actually, a lot of them were in distress. But not all of them."

"The reason we have the two trees is because I guess some hippy guy hung a hammock between them in an effort to save them."

"A hippy guy?" Jill's gray eyes widened.

"That's the way we heard the story. When we moved in, we were told that this wild hippy guy camped out between the trees and stopped the bulldozer from knocking them down. The builders worked around him, and the trees are still there."

Jill looked as if that was the best news she had heard all day. "I can't believe this. Those two trees are in your yard?"

"Yes. They're nice and healthy, huge and full of oranges every year. I'm so glad that loony guy put up his hammock." I leaned back, trying to read Jill's expression. "I'm sure you must have heard that story before."

"As a matter of fact I have," Jill said. "That loony guy, by the way, was my husband."

Three

Both my hands flew to cover my face, as the waitress brought my mocha latte and placed it on the table in front of me. Without looking at Jill between my closed fingers, I said, "I am so sorry! I can't believe I said that."

Jill laughed and reached over to pull away my fingers. "It's okay. Ray *was* a hippy in those days. And he's been called worse than loony, so don't worry about that either."

"Well, then I'll say this with all sincerity." I put my hands in my lap and leaned forward. "Because of your husband, I have eagerly opened my windows every spring for the past twenty years, and our whole house has filled with the fragrance of orange blossoms. He did a wonderful thing saving those trees. I'm the one who has enjoyed the reward of his zeal."

"The reward of his zeal," Jill repeated. She teared up, and I felt bad for making her cry again. Swallowing hard, she paused before saying, "Thank you for telling me that today. It means a lot."

Feeling hesitant to say anything else, I sipped my mocha and glanced at Jill's tears as they wandered over her lower lids and silently rolled down to her chin.

"Ray and I met in high school." She looked out the window. "Ray was really something back in the seventies. Every mother's nightmare of the kind of guy she didn't want her daughter to bring home. Long hair, leather sandals. He was ready to protest injustice anytime and anywhere."

Jill's moist cheeks lifted as she smiled and turned back to face me. "I was a goody-goody and a cheerleader, which was a combination that Ray found irresistible, or so he always said. He was determined to win me over, and once Ray Radovich put his mind to something, well…you might as well give up opposing him."

I nodded my understanding. "My husband, Tony, is the same way. He and I met in the parking lot at a concert. We started talking as we were walking in, and then we sat next to each other. That was it. We were pretty much together after that."

"What concert?"

I hesitated slightly before answering. I didn't know if telling Jill that Tony and I had met at a Christian concert would polarize us. I'd experienced that sort of distancing from women at work who were friendly and open toward me until they found out I was a Christian and very involved at church. Their assumptions about me took over at that point, and they pulled away, as if I were on a campaign to convert them instead of to become their friend. I didn't want that to happen with Jill.

Nevertheless, I was a Christian and not ashamed to say so. That's who I was, and I couldn't pretend otherwise.

"Tony and I met at a Christian concert. A church in Costa

Mesa used to have free concerts every Saturday night and—"

"Yes! In a circus tent, right? It was out in a bean field or strawberry field. Not far from South Coast Plaza. You went there, too? Ray and I went every week after we became Christians our senior year of high school."

My mouth dropped open, and I shook my head in amazement. I was thrilled to hear Jill say she was also a Christian. "That means we could have been at the same concerts, because Tony and I used to go all the time, too! Can you imagine?"

"We might have even sat next to each other but never met."

Jill and I ran through a list of the most memorable music groups and came to the conclusion that we definitely were at least in the same place on the same nights.

"You have no idea what this means to me right now," Jill said. "Meeting you, finding out you're a believer, talking about home and Ray and high school days…" She choked up and reached for my hand to give it a squeeze. "This is the best thing that could have happened to me today."

"Me, too," I echoed, giving her hand a squeeze back. I wished I could express to her how sincerely I meant it.

"I only live a few blocks away. I knew I had to get out of the house today. It took me all morning to pull myself together because…" She reached for a napkin to dab her tears and didn't finish her thought.

She didn't need to. I understood more than she could imagine. "I know what you're feeling, Jill. It's okay. You're going to be okay."

It struck me that I didn't know exactly what she was feeling. I only knew what I was feeling. The reassurance was more for me than it was for Jill. We were both going to be okay. I just knew it.

She looked out the window and then back at me with a soft expression. "I didn't know what I needed today. All I knew was that I had to get out of the house. Now I know why."

Again I nodded my understanding.

"There's something Ray used to say about answered prayer: 'If you feel a deep hunger but don't know what you want, just ask God to order for you. That way you'll always get whatever is the best on the menu.'"

I started to leak my own sorry tears and chased them with a silent confession. I had spent the last week so lost in myself and unresponsive to God that I hadn't asked Him to order anything for me. Yet He still gave me exactly what I needed to fill the emptiness.

"God is so good to us," I said in a whisper.

Jill's nod was slow in coming, but when her head began to bob, a trickle of laughter followed. "I feel like we're in high school again. I can't control any of my emotions."

"I know." I fanned myself as I felt my temperature spiking. "And I think I'm starting to have hot flashes." Lowering my voice I leaned closer and asked, "Forty-five is pretty young for this, isn't it?"

"Not necessarily. Stress can really mess up your body's rhythm."

Our conversation turned to details about our bodies, and the pros and cons of hormone therapy. After that we slid into other girls-only topics. For the next hour, our heads were bent close as we did what clear-hearted women do so well. We opened the door, let each other come in, and warmed ourselves by the fire of our spirits.

That's when I realized that my new "home" in this place of upside-down living wasn't an ugly garage with a blazing bedspread and defiled bathtub. My home was my heart. And today, at last, my home was clean and ready for company.

As the afternoon light dimmed, Jill looked at her watch. "Do you need to get home soon?"

"No, not really. What about you?"

Jill shook her head and in a thin voice said, "No one is at my house waiting for me."

"I know what you mean. Tony hasn't yet come home early enough for us to eat dinner together." With a sigh I added, "I think I have a bad case of DENS."

"What's that?"

"Delayed Empty Nest Syndrome."

"I don't think I've ever heard of that," Jill said.

"Me neither. I just made it up!"

We laughed, and I told Jill how our home had been Grand Central for many years. We had only one daughter, but she had many friends, and our place seemed to be the designated hang-out.

"What about you? Do you and Ray have children?"

She held up three fingers. "All boys. Or I should say *men*. The two oldest are both married and settled in California. James, our youngest, is going to Victoria University here in Wellington, but he moved into student housing at the term change. It's been very quiet around my house since he left."

"I know what you mean. We had exchange students living with us the first two years Skyler was in high school, and her senior year my nephew moved in and stayed until this past Christmas. As soon as he moved out, we remodeled the kitchen, but that was barely done before we came here. I'm not used to being alone."

"It's not so great, is it?"

"The only advantage seems to be there's a lot less laundry." My quip reminded me of the clothes I'd left hanging on the line. I told Jill I'd better head back to take down the clothes before the sun set. I could imagine all of Tony's jeans turning stiff in the cooling air.

"Is there anything you need to help you get settled? Groceries? Anything for your house?"

"No, our apartment is too small to even hold the things we shipped over."

"Let me know if you think of anything. Anything at all." She wrote down her phone number, and we agreed to meet here again next Tuesday for coffee.

"Unless," Jill added, as we rose and were heading for the door, "you think of anything you want or need, and then we could squeeze in a shopping trip."

"I actually wouldn't mind a new bedspread."

"Then let's go find you a bedspread. What does tomorrow look like for you?"

Our plans were quickly formulated, and Jill asked if I wanted to look for anything besides a bedspread.

"I don't think so. To be honest, I shouldn't be making such a big deal about this bedspread. Tony thinks I should be able to endure this one for three months, but it's really obnoxious."

"Three months?" Jill stopped walking out of the café and looked at me. "Why do you only have to endure it for three months?"

"Tony's position at the studio is for three months."

"It is? Then what?"

"Then we go back to California."

Jill looked surprised.

"Didn't I say something earlier about this being a tempo-rary position?"

"If you did, I didn't catch it. And that is possible, with all the laughing and crying we were doing. But seriously, three months isn't long enough."

"Not long enough for what?" Ever since we arrived I'd been counting the days until we could leave, and now Jill was telling me our stay was going to be too short.

Before Jill could give me the answer that seemed to be for-mulating in her mind, we were interrupted by the sound of a long, flat car horn. We were standing outside the Chocolate Fish, and apparently we were blocking a prime parking spot. We hopped out of the way.

"Excuse us," I muttered with plenty of sarcasm.

"Don't worry." Jill waved at the driver. "It's Tracey. She's a permanent fixture here at the café."

A petite, energetic woman with very short, very red hair hopped out of a vehicle that made me stop and stare. The 1952 classic Chevy truck had a rounded hood and roof, and lots of shiny chrome on the front grille and bumper. The buffed-to-a-shine paint was sunshine yellow. Someone had taken good care of that little gem.

"Hallo!" The woman came toward us all smiles and gave Jill a hug.

"Tracey, this is Kathy Salerno. She just moved here. Her husband is at Jackamond. You won't believe this, but it's like we had parallel lives in high school, but we never met until today. We've spent the whole afternoon comparing our lives."

Tracey greeted me with an unexpected hug. "You both had to come all the way to Kiwi Land before you could meet each other inside my little café. Lovely! Welcome, Kathy!"

I wasn't used to being called Kathy. I'd always been Kathleen. The more lighthearted Kathy had never been activated, because I viewed that as a name reserved for the popular girls—the cheerleaders and homecoming queens.

With a lump in my throat, I realized that Jill had renamed me. In this new place of global turnabouts, I was being accepted as one of the popular girls by Jill, a former cheerleader, and Tracey, a rich girl with a cool car.

"Your truck is gorgeous." I felt a little nervous that I might say the wrong thing and be banished from the group. "My uncle used to refurbish old trucks. He would have loved this one."

"We call her Beatrice the Dazzling Bumblebee," Tracey said. "Bea for short."

"She's a honey, all right." I hadn't realized I'd made a bee-related pun, but Tracey laughed generously.

"Did your uncle let you drive his refurbished trucks?"

"No, never."

Tracey glanced at Jill and then back at me with a mischievous glimmer in her eyes. "Then you'll have to take Bea for a spin to make up for lost opportunities." She held the car keys out to me and gave them a jingle.

I looked at Jill. Her expression told me that not every visitor to the Chocolate Fish was extended such an offer. I felt as if this was part of my initiation to the cool girls' club.

"Are you sure?" I asked.

"Of course. Come on. It's a perfect evening for a drive."

I bravely headed for what my brain said was the driver's side. Tracey was right behind me, chuckling and saying, "Other side. You're the driver."

"Oh, of course!" I laughed nervously, my American ways showing through.

I peered into the cab and saw the steering wheel was huge, and as soon as I settled in behind it, I discovered it had a lot of "play."

I took my position with a thrill I don't think I'd ever felt, even when I was in high school. I had been a goody-goody like Jill. I played it safe, taking very few risks. Driving someone's "honey bee" down what felt was the wrong side of the road wasn't a huge risk as opposed to, say, bungee jumping. But for me, this was a nerve-wracking leap into thin air.

My heart was pounding as Tracey pointed out the gears on the steering column and reminded me to put in the clutch with my left foot before shifting. A pullout button on the front panel adjusted the throttle.

"And you say you never drove one of your uncle's vintage trucks? Not even when he wasn't looking?"

"No, this is all new to me."

"Well, Bob's your uncle," Tracey said.

"Actually, my uncle's name was Harry."

Tracey gave me a strange look, and then her face lit up and she laughed, as if I had just made another clever joke.

"No, Bob's your uncle," she repeated. "We say that here. *Bob's your uncle.* You don't say that?"

Jill leaned over with a dozen giggles sparkling in her eyes. "It took me a while to get used to that expression, too. It's like we would say, 'There you have it' or 'There you go.'"

"*Bob's your uncle?*" I repeated. "That makes no sense. Where in the world do you suppose that saying came from?"

Tracey flicked away a giggle-tear. "Guess we can't blame that one on the Americans. Go ahead and start up Bea. What's the saying where you come from? Surf City, here we come."

Jill applauded. "We will take credit for that saying, since we are a couple of California girls."

Tracey sang off tune, *"I wish they all could be California girls!"*

We laughed again, but as soon as the merriment dissolved, I felt the return of my nervousness about being behind the wheel of this imposing Queen Bee. With the mirrors adjusted and my feet in position, I turned the key, and the eager engine rumbled to life. My left hand was in place, ready to shift gears with a lever on our car that I would have used for the windshield wipers.

"Go for it, Kathy!" Jill cheered.

"Stay to the left," Tracey reminded me.

Easing off the clutch and giving Bea a thimbleful of nectar, I inched us away from the front of the café.

"Don't be afraid of her. Go ahead, drive like you mean it," Tracey said, as I picked up speed and headed for the right lane. "Stay left!"

"Oh, right"

"No, left," Tracey repeated.

"Right," I agreed. "Left."

"Just drive," Jill said with a giggle. "Keep the dividing line on your side of the car, and you'll be fine."

"Got it." I attempted a less-than-smooth shift into second gear and could almost feel the startled engine working with me to make the adjustments.

"She doesn't need much coaxing," Tracey said. "You're doing fine."

In an effort to stay in my lane, I overcompensated with the large steering wheel and promptly rolled up over the curb. A burst of nervous laughter spilled out, and I turned too far to the right before veering back to where I should be.

"You have the feel for her now," Tracey said. "Where to?"

"Why don't you drive back to your place, Kathy?" Jill suggested. "That way I'll know where to pick you up in the morning for our shopping trip."

"Shopping plans already, girls? Good for you."

"Do you want to come with us, Tracey?"

"Ask me another time. Tomorrow is a busy day at the café."

I kept my hands at ten and two o'clock on the leather-wrapped steering wheel and felt confident I could find our place, since I knew it was on the same road. All I had to do was keep this buggy pointed in the same direction for less than a kilometer, and we'd be there.

"Third." Tracey tapped my leg.

I knew she meant it was time to shift into third, and I did so with impressive smoothness.

"Well done!" Tracey praised.

I grinned. "Oh, yeah? Then where's my chocolate fish?"

Tracey laughed. "Very good! She catches on quickly, doesn't she?"

Jill laughed too, and somehow I knew I'd made it through this self-imposed initiation ceremony. I was cruising down the road like one of the cool girls now, head cheerleader, homecoming queen, brimming with glee and filled with pride.

And you know what they say pride comes before…

Exactly.

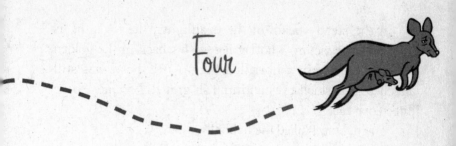

Four

As we motored down the road, I squinted to see out the window. In the glow of twilight, the houses I'd walked past earlier that afternoon now looked different. Just when I thought I recognized Mr. Barry's house ahead on the left, Tracey spouted, "Look out for the pizza delivery boy!"

I spotted a guy on the right, steering his bike with one hand and precariously balancing a pizza box in his other hand.

"Hey, that's—"

"Kathy, stay to the left!"

In an immediate response to Tracey's shouted warning, I cranked the steering wheel to the left, then back to the right, and then way too far to the left. This time my overcorrection popped us up over the curb, heading for a garden of mums. I slammed on the brakes, but it was too little, too late. All three of us winced and then shrieked as we heard and felt the deep thud of obvious impact with something in our path.

"What did we hit?" Jill was the first one out of the car. Tracey and I were right behind her.

In the steady beam of the headlights, the three of us peered at the victim, who lay flat on his back in the golden flowers. I drew in a horrified breath. His head was still attached. His small eyes and impish grin still seemed to be directed at me.

"The hobbit. I killed the hobbit!"

"Don't say that too loud," Tracey said. "It could be considered a national crime. Besides, I think he's okay. Help me get him back up."

"Kathleen?" Tony's voice coming toward us was accompanied by the faint scent of pepperoni.

Tracey whispered. "Did you order a pizza?"

"No, that's my husband."

Tracey and Jill snapped into formation beside me with their backs to the fallen hobbit.

"Hallo," Tracey said with calm cheerfulness.

"Good evening," Jill added, playing along with the innocent adolescent routine.

"Lovely evening, isn't it?" Tracey asked.

"Kathleen?" Tony looked at me, as if he still couldn't compute this extreme makeover from couch potato to highway hellion.

"Tony, these are my new friends, Jill and Tracey."

"Hi." He nodded and returned his incredulous stare to me. "Are you...are you okay?"

"Sure, I'm fine! We were just, you know, out driving around in Tracey's truck, and I parked kind of funny."

"You were driving?"

I nodded like a bobble-head doll riding down a bumpy road at fifty miles per hour.

Tony's expression was difficult to decipher. Was he still

stunned or was that boyish amusement on his face? "I, ah, I got a pizza for us," he said. "There's plenty. Tracey, Jill, if you want to come in and have some, you're welcome to join us."

"Thanks, but I have to get back to the café," Tracey said.

"I should be going as well," Jill said without moving.

"Okay. Well, nice meeting you both. Good night," Tony said.

"Good night," Jill said.

"Cheers!" Tracey peeped.

Despite our farewells, the three of us cruisin' chicks hadn't moved. I was hoping Tony would take the hint and go inside so we could get the hobbit back on his huge, hairy feet again. I was also hoping Mr. Barry wasn't home, or if he was, that he hadn't heard us or looked out to see what was going on.

"I guess I'll, ah…I'll take the pizza inside and see you in a few minutes, Kathleen."

"Okay."

"Well, good evening, ladies."

"Good evening," Jill and Tracey repeated in unison. The three of us inched our way to the right with synchronized steps. We had to keep our human shield at the proper angle so Tony wouldn't see the horizontal Frodo.

As soon as we heard the side door of the garage close, we turned and went to work putting everything back in order, trying hard not to let our giggles escalate to rowdy laughter.

"That was close," Tracey whispered.

Jill giggled. "I can't believe us! I haven't acted like that since…"

"Since far too long," Tracey concluded for her. "I'd almost forgotten what a great laugh you have, Jill. It's made my day seeing you like this. Kathy, you're the best!"

As Tracey was praising me, I was crouched down examining

the grille of her truck to see if I'd done any damage to her beautiful Beatrice. "You might be a little hasty with your kind words, Tracey. Look, I dented the grille."

She leaned close. "No, that was already there."

"Are you sure?"

"Of course I'm sure. You'd have to be a lot more aggressive than you were to damage this baby. Not that I'm inviting you to be more aggressive next time you take her for a spin."

"Don't worry. I don't think I'll be imposing myself on poor Bea anytime soon."

"And why not? Now that you've gotten used to her, she and I will let you drive her anytime you want."

"Tracey, you are so gracious."

"Aren't I, though?" The soft glow of the headlights brightened her whimsical expression as she gave me a hug. "Next time you come into the café, I'll have a chocolate fish waiting for you. You too, Jill. And don't stay away so long this time."

"I won't." Jill reached over to give my arm a squeeze before she climbed back in the car with Tracey. "See you tomorrow."

I nodded and waved. Tracey started up the engine. Bea seemed to slip into a contented buzz now that Tracey was behind the wheel.

Entering our apartment, I found Tony standing in the center of the room looking at me with his new, mysterious expression on his face.

"So that really was you outside."

"Yes, it really was me. The new, improved me."

"You know what I did?" Tony asked. "I actually walked in here and checked to see if you were in the bathtub."

"Why would I be in the bathtub?"

"Why would you be driving around town in a vintage

automobile with a couple of shrieking women and knocking down ornamental lawn fixtures?"

"Oh. You saw that?"

"I didn't actually see it, but I couldn't help but notice how the three of you were acting; so I added up two plus two."

Math. Math had never done anything good for me. Although, I have to admit that today, for the first time in a long time, I didn't feel as if my life was half over with only the boring part left. Today I felt as if the second half could hold more freedom to do the sorts of things I'd never had time for before. It was pretty fun not to feel responsible for everyone else in the family and to take a silly risk by getting behind the wheel of Beatrice.

"How bad is he?" Tony asked.

"Frodo? He's fine."

"The flowers?"

"Mum's the word!"

Tony stared at me without blinking.

I couldn't stop laughing. "Mum's the word," I repeated just in case Tony hadn't heard my joke the first time. He certainly wasn't as quick at picking up jokes as Tracey had been.

Tony gave me a long, sunken-eyebrow sort of examination. "Kathleen, are you taking some sort of medication that I don't know about?"

That deduction really cracked me up. "No! As a matter of fact, this is the first day since we've been here that I haven't taken a single pill. Not for a headache or a stomachache or sinus pressure. I'm finally all the way here, Tony. I know my body arrived on the plane two weeks ago, but the rest of me finally caught up."

At last my husband looked as if he was willing to accept

the new me. We sat down to eat the cooled pizza, and I gave him a thorough recounting of what had happened since he had left me earlier that day.

When I reached the end of my tale, I asked Tony what he thought of inviting Jill and her husband over sometime soon for dinner or at least coffee.

"Sure, it's a great idea. Did I tell you I cleared it with Mad Dog to take one of the vans tomorrow? I thought you and I could go do something."

"Tony, I told Jill I'd go shopping with her tomorrow. I'm going to look for a new bedspread."

"This one really bothers you, doesn't it?"

I glanced over at my vivid nemesis and was shocked when the first thought that came to mind was, *I guess it's not so bad.* Apparently everything around me was looking better now that I had my equilibrium back.

"Can you borrow the studio van a different day?" I asked.

"Sure. And if you're not going to be home tomorrow, I'll go in to work. I was trying to find ways to make you more comfortable here."

I thought Tony looked relieved that he didn't have two full-time jobs: one at the studio and the other at home trying to keep me from flipping out. I didn't know if I liked the idea of his agreeing to overtime and working on Saturdays, but I did like being his companion and counterpart again instead of his patient and sometimes opponent.

I fell asleep that night in my husband's arms, dreaming up plans for how Jill, Ray, Tony, and I could all fit in our apartment for a cozy dinner party. Or maybe with our limited space and furniture it would just be appetizers.

The next morning I was up before Tony, getting ready for

my shopping trip with Jill. I fumbled around looking for clean undies and realized I'd left the laundry on the line all night.

Dashing into the backyard in my pajamas, I was met by a steady morning drizzle. All our clothes were as wet as when I'd hung them out the day before. The drying rack in the bathtub became my only hope. The rack and the hair dryer. I stood shivering, my bare feet on the cold tile floor and my nose dripping while I shot hot air at my unmentionables.

Despite that setback, I was dressed and ready to go by ten o'clock. Although my elastic waistband was still a little damp. I missed my clothes dryer. I missed it even more than I missed my morning Cheerios, and I dearly missed Cheerios. A few days earlier Tony had brought home some Weet-Bix, a popular cereal, according to the guys at work. To me it tasted like Shredded Wheat without any sugar. My hunt was still on for a breakfast food that I would look forward to every morning.

Tony had a bowl of Weet-Bix and left on his bike before Jill arrived. I noticed that the sun had come out. The gentle world outside the door smelled fresh, new, and green. I could smell a dozen different foliage fragrances than the ones distinguishable in southern California. The warm, sweet, tropical scents mixed with the deep smells of an evergreen forest.

I ventured outside, wondering if I should take a chance and hang out the clothes again. I decided it was worth a try. As soon as I had all the damp clothes back on the line, I walked around to the front of the house and nonchalantly examined the mums. I was happy to see that the rainy night had worked wonders in covering the tire marks in the previously flattened grass. Only a few stems near the statue were snapped off. The hobbit looked no worse after his tumble.

I felt a soft poke from something in my jeans pocket.

Putting my hand in, I expected to find a pin of some sort but instead discovered the two white-tipped feathers I'd pulled from my hair yesterday when I had met Jill. With a smile, I returned to the apartment and tucked the feathers into a small plastic bag. My mind kicked into gear, and I mentally started to design a homemade card for Jill that featured two feathers on the front.

Grabbing a notepad, I jotted down possible lines for the inside.

Friends of a feather sip lattes together.

For my fine, feather friend. I appreciate you a latte.

So glad I fluttered your way. You made the day fly by.

With a silly streak rising I wrote,

When we're together, mum's the word.

The mum joke didn't sound as funny as it had last night, so I tried another route. But the sound of a car in the gravel driveway interrupted my creative writing spell. I quickly penned a final madcap line,

Spending time with you could become hobbit-forming.

Five

"I see you decided to park in a more conventional spot than the one I chose last night." I greeted Jill with my hand up, shielding my eyes from the sun. It was strange watching Jill exit the "passenger's" side of her compact car.

"Good morning," she said in a tone that was much more subdued than I felt. I wanted to ask if she was okay, but she was the first to ask a question.

"Is Tony here?"

"No, he went to work."

"Would you mind if we went inside and talked before we go shopping?"

"No." I tried to stay lighthearted. "You can have a look at the bedspread and tell me if you think I'm loco for trying to replace it."

We went inside, and Jill diplomatically said, "I've seen worse." Looking around she added, "This is a nice apartment."

"It's tiny."

"But it's clean. Everything looks new. I'm sure you were told how difficult it is to find reasonable housing."

I nodded and led the way to the other room. She agreed that the bathtub was a bonus. Having Jill's positive input made me feel better about the apartment. It's amazing how a few sincere, affirming words from a woman you admire can change your opinion about something.

"Would you like a cup of tea?" I pulled out the box of tea bags from the packed kitchen cupboard.

"Sure. Thanks."

"It's not fancy tea."

"Gumboot is fine."

"Actually, the box says 'Bell Tea.' Is that okay?" I held it up so she could see the limitations of my hospitality and have a chance to decline the offer if she wanted.

"I'm sorry. I didn't mean to confuse you. Gumboot around here is what they call plain black tea. It's different than something like Earl Grey or green tea."

"So is Bell Tea a Gumboot tea?"

"Yes, and I would love a cup. Thanks, Kathy."

"Do you take cream or sugar?"

"A little of both would be nice."

"That's just the way I like my tea, too."

Yesterday Jill and I had slipped easily into the role of high school best friends. Today, in my ridiculously tiny, Susie Homemaker kitchen with my Easy-Bake Oven and box of Bell Tea, I felt as if we were playing little girls having a tea party. I almost wished I had decorated sugar cubes to offer instead of an unimaginative box of granulated white sugar.

"Mind if I use your bathroom?" Jill asked.

"Help yourself." With a tease I added, "Let me know if you have trouble finding it."

Jill wasn't laughing at any of my jokes. I decided to stop trying to be clever and to direct my efforts into putting together a nice tea party. To fancy up the sugar, I poured some into a freshly washed small bowl I'd found in the silverware drawer that I think was supposed to be for teriyaki sauce. Finding a fancy container for the milk was a bigger challenge. I decided the glass milk bottle would have to work. Tony had become enamored with the "old-fashioned" glass bottles as soon as he discovered them at the dairy, and we now had two.

I remembered the snapped-off mums I'd tossed in the trash bin the night before as we tidied up the scene of the crime. Rifling through the rubbish, I pulled them out and gave them a good rinse in the sink and a shake before transforming one of the empty milk bottles into a vase.

With my little tea party ready at the table, I poured the boiling water over the tea bags in our two yellow mugs.

"I have some cookies," I told Jill as she took her place at the table. "Unless you think it's too early for cookies."

"It's never too early for cookies. Especially Toffee Pops. Have you had these yet? They're one of my favorites."

I looked at the package in my hand. "I don't think I've tried these." I arranged several of the small, round, chocolate-covered cookies on a plate.

"This is wonderful," Jill said. "Nice touch with the flowers."

"Those are the ones from last night. Broken, thrown away, but look! I pulled them out, and they still have plenty of life and color in them."

Joining Jill, I placed the cookies on our table, and we had just enough room left for a folded napkin and a spoon.

"Well, this answers my question," I said, trying to rearrange the items in the limited space.

"What question is that?"

"Last night I told Tony we probably would have to settle for an appetizer party instead of a dinner party when we have you and Ray over. As you can see, we don't even have four chairs."

Jill's expression fell. She put down her cup of tea, and the stream of tears I'd seen on her face yesterday returned.

"Are you okay? Did I say something that upset you?"

"Kathy, I hardly know how to tell you this. I wish I'd said something yesterday."

"That's okay. You can tell me now."

"I need to apologize."

"Apologize for what?"

"When we met, I think I dropped into some sort of parallel reality. It felt so good that I stayed there a little too long."

"Yesterday was great fun," I agreed. "It was a little wacky once we got in Tracey's car, but there's nothing to apologize for."

"No, Kathy. Just listen, okay?"

I nodded and kept my mouth shut.

"It's about Ray. I would love for you to meet Ray. I would give anything if he and I could come join you and Tony for dinner sometime. But we won't be able to do that because, you see, my husband is gone."

"Oh, Jill!" I felt instant anger toward Ray. How could any man leave a woman as wonderful as Jill?

"It was two years ago yesterday, and that's why I went to

the Chocolate Fish. I needed to get out of the house." She let out a puff of breath and whispered, "Last year I spent the anniversary of his funeral at home alone, and I knew I didn't want to do that again."

I was so stunned I couldn't speak.

"I'm sorry, Kathy. I should have said something. It wasn't fair not to let you know. I meant to tell you. But then we started talking about Ray and high school, and in a strange way it seemed as if he wasn't really gone. And that was the nicest feeling I'd had in, well, two years."

"Oh, Jill."

A crooked smile kept her lips from trembling as she went on. "Being with you and thinking about Ray was such a sweet gift to me. You invited me to talk about Ray—to say his name without connecting it to his death. When you did that, something inside me started to heal. It was such a wonderful sensation to finally feel that healing. I couldn't bring myself to tell you the truth. So I let you believe what wasn't true. I am sorry, Kathy."

"Jill, it's okay. You don't have to apologize."

I went for a box of tissues and pulled my chair up next to hers. "I can't imagine what this has been like for you."

A few quiet moments passed before she said, "At first, I had a lot of support from people around me. They were there through the whole ordeal. So many people did so much to help me. But now they don't ask about Ray. Nobody talks about him. It's as if he vanished, and everyone has forgotten him. The worst part is that since Ray doesn't exist for some people anymore, that means I don't exist either. I've become the invisible widow of the great Ray Radovich. They don't see me."

I handed her another tissue.

"But you! Kathy, yesterday you saw me. You brought back my loony, youthful, hippy guy, and he was still alive to you. More than that, I was alive to you."

"Oh, Jill," I said with all the tenderness I felt in my heart. "You are alive. Very much alive. You're not invisible at all." After that, I didn't know what to say, so I put my arm around her shoulders, and together we swayed back and forth until all the tears were gone.

We didn't end up shopping that day. Instead, we talked for a long time over our tea and cookies and then drove to a lookout on Mount Victoria. Jill said I had given her a broader view of her life, and now she wanted to give me a broader view of the world I was living in. We parked in an open lot and climbed to a fortified lookout spot. Lush, green grass skirted the hilltop where several visitors had stretched out to take in the incredible view. Below us, on the many hills of Wellington, rose and fell thousands of rooftops like bits of red, brown, and gray tiles scattered across the green. Where the green ended, the soft blues began—either the blue of the ocean and the bay or the blue of the cloudless sky.

The wind began to push us around, taunting my ponytail, daring it to whip around and slap me across the mouth. Jill's golden locks were flipping out at ear level the way Marilyn Monroe's skirt flipped out in the photo of her standing over the air grate.

"What a view!" I called across to Jill.

She nodded and pointed out the airport, far below us. To our right was the bay, lined with tall buildings. In every direction we turned, we saw houses. Wellington was much larger and more spread out than I'd realized.

"Do you see the large ferry there in the harbor? That one goes to Picton on the South Island of New Zealand."

"How far away is the South Island?"

"The ferry takes about three hours to Picton. Maybe three and a half. If the weather is nice, it's a beautiful crossing."

"And how far away is Christchurch?"

"It's at least six or seven hours south of Picton. They have a train that goes from Picton to Christchurch. It's considered one of the most picturesque train rides in the world."

"Have you taken it?"

"No. We planned to once, when Ray's mom was visiting us. She didn't do well on the ferry crossing, though. The trip was stormy, and none of us felt like taking a long train ride after that. We spent the night in Picton and flew home the next morning."

"And you haven't been back to the South Island since then?"

"No. I'd like to go. Especially to Christchurch. Everyone says the town has a quaint, British feel."

"That's what Tony said. He suggested I take a tour there," I said.

"It's a nice time of year to go. Not too many tourists. It's the final outpost for all the major explorations to Antarctica. Did you know that?"

"No. How far south is it?"

"I don't know how far south it is, but think of it this way: Wellington is more or less in the middle of New Zealand. Auckland is at the top of the North Island and closer to the equator."

"Okay, I'm with you so far."

"And then Christchurch is at the other end of New Zealand on the South Island."

We started walking back to the car, both speculating on what the weather would be like now in Christchurch. Once inside, instead of starting the engine, Jill and I settled in and quietly looked out at the incredible bird's-eye view of the city. The wind raced through the lookout parking lot. All the world seemed to be spread out before us, colorfully painted with endless possibilities. It was a new world to me in many ways. One I was ready to embrace.

"You know," Jill said after our comfortable pause. "If you really want to go to Christchurch, let me know. I'd like to go sometime."

"With a tour group?"

"Not particularly."

"Me neither."

"Maybe we could go on a Sisterchicks adventure, just the two of us."

"A Sisterchicks adventure?" I repeated. "What's that?"

"That's what my daughter-in-law calls a weekend getaway. She and her best friend take one every year and call it their Sisterchicks adventure. I always thought it would be fun to do something like that. Ray and I used to travel together a lot, but I can't remember ever taking off with a girlfriend for a vacation."

"I've never gotten away like that, either," I said. "Tony told me I should do some exploring, but I didn't want to go by myself. It would be lots of fun to go with you."

"I think so, too. We can book our tickets on-line."

"Okay. Although I'll have to ask Tony to book mine at work because, as you may have noticed, I don't have a computer at home. Or a telephone. Or a television. But I have a refrigerator."

"And a bathtub," Jill reminded me.

"Yes, I have a nice bathtub. It's just that I haven't yet figured out how to get my bathtub or my refrigerator to connect to the Internet to book airline tickets."

Jill laughed. Like Tracey said the day before, Jill had a great laugh. Just getting close to her bubbly laugh made me want to join in.

"If you want, we can stop by my house after this and use my computer. But first we have one more place of interest to see." Jill started the engine.

"If it's the Embassy Theatre, I've already seen it," I said flatly.

"You know about the Embassy?"

"I didn't before Mad Dog drove us past on our way from the airport."

Jill stepped on the brakes and looked at me. "Mad Dog?"

"That's Tony's boss. Do you know him?"

She paused before saying, "Yes, I know Mad Dog."

Jill continued to back the car out of the parking lot. From her response to Mad Dog's name, I guessed Jill didn't have a good impression of him. Even though I knew he could have done plenty to earn his reputation with Jill, I felt the need to defend him—or at least to explain the nickname.

"Did you know that his real name is Marcus? My husband gave him the nickname at a studio party years ago. They did a commercial involving a high-strung poodle that kept chasing its tail instead of cooperating with the film crew. Tony took footage of the tail-chaser that they couldn't use, turned it into a clip, and set it up as a screen saver on Marcus's computer. After that Marcus got to be a little too good at imitating the poodle, especially as an icebreaker at parties."

"Oh," Jill said politely.

The topic of Mad Dog seemed to hang between us like an embarrassing pair of jumbo briefs on the invisible clothesline of our forming friendship. I decided not to bring up any more stories about Mad Dog.

Jill was the one who changed the subject. "Kathy, I want to thank you for something you said yesterday. It really helped me."

"What did I say?"

"When you were talking about Ray stringing the hammock between the orange trees, you said you had experienced the 'reward of his zeal.' I love that."

"It's true."

"I know." She glanced at me and then back at the road. "And you know what? I needed to hear that. Thank you."

"You're welcome."

We coasted a little farther down the road on the side of Mount Victoria, and Jill revealed she was taking me to see a famous movie spot.

"I should warn you that I'm not extremely reverent about *Lord of the Rings*. You saw what I did to the hobbit in the garden."

"You'll like this place," Jill assured me. "And even if you don't, please just pretend you're impressed because it's a special place for me. I was there the day they filmed, because Ray got special permission and…well, I'll just show you."

Jill pulled the car to the side of the road and turned off the engine. We got out and walked along what looked like a hiking trail that led into a densely wooded area. The dirt trail was covered with a carpet of dried, brown pine needles that cushioned our steps.

"This *is* beautiful," I said.

"I told you."

I stopped to touch the thick bark on one of the towering giants. "These trees are so old. They're ancient. Look at this trunk."

"I know." Jill nodded. "This is a wonderful place, isn't it?"

"It's amazing."

"Look how gnarled some of these trees are." She pointed to a particularly unusual tree. "You can almost see faces in the trunks. And look over there. The moss seems iridescent."

"Wow."

The farther we walked, the more enchanting the forest became. Sunlight slid through the high canopy of thick branches and seemed to ignite clumps of grass into vibrant green campfires, clustered in the open spaces. All across the forest floor, these emerald patches blazed with a natural glory that hinted at the hidden glimmers still tucked away in God's imagination.

"Right here." Jill stopped, and I tried to see what she was pointing at.

Six

Jill pointed to where the trail took a sudden dip. An outgrowth of lanky tree roots was exposed by erosion.

"Try to picture this spot with another tree they brought in and put right here. It was a tree they made in the props department. Any idea what scene they were filming?"

I sized up the setting.

"I'll give you a hint. It was when the hobbits left the Shire."

I looked around, and suddenly I could visualize it. "This is where Frodo and his pals hid, isn't it?"

"That's right." Jill moved to the trail's edge. "Right here."

"I remember that scene! The hobbits jumped off the road and hid under these massive roots. Right here! That's so cool!"

"You got it."

"And those dark horses came through here on the trail."

"The ring on the chain around Frodo's neck was calling out to the Ringwraiths."

"I can see it all. Wow! They didn't need to add many props, did they?"

"No." Jill was smiling. She seemed to be drinking in sweet memories of the place. No evil spirits on black horses were riding through her mind, as she gazed down the trail. "That was the first scene they filmed, and the rest of the project unfolded from that day."

We stood alone on the pine needle–padded trail, and I knew where I'd bring Tony the next time he borrowed the studio's van.

"Have I made a fan out of you yet?"

"Almost." I moved to the trail's edge, sizing up the hollowed-out spot.

"Kathy, what are you doing?"

"Come on, let's try it out. I'm not exactly hobbit-size, but I think we can fit."

Jill laughed. "You have to be kidding!"

"No, I'm serious. Come on!"

We were dressed in Saturday shopping clothes, but who cared? Edging over the side of the trail, we grabbed on to the extended tree roots and used them like a climber would use a rope.

"That looks roomy enough." I pointed to the largest hollowed-out area under the tree.

"This is the craziest thing I've done since…"

"Since you went driving with me yesterday? Come on, we can fit in there."

And indeed we did. We fit so well that the dampness from the rich, dark earth penetrated our clothes. I twitched at the thought of legions of creepy, crawly creatures jumping on me, as if I were their bus ride out of there.

"Listen," Jill said, holding her breath. We heard the steady pounding of feet coming our way.

"Joggers," Jill whispered.

"Should we jump out and scare them?" I whispered.

Jill covered her mouth so her giggles wouldn't escape. "I can't believe we're doing this."

"On the count of three," I whispered. "One, two, three!"

Instead of springing out of hiding like two slender, annoyingly perky cheerleaders, the width of our midlife frames wedged us together at the opening, and Jill's shirt caught on a protruding twig.

"Wait! I don't want to tear this shirt. Hang on." She tried to pull her right arm around to use both hands to release her shirt. In the flurry, my long hair caught on the buttons that ran up the sleeve of her cute shirt.

"Ow! Stop! Wait! Now I'm caught."

"Are you two okay?" One of the joggers stood looking down on us, his face expressing surprise. It just wasn't the same surprise effect we were trying for.

"We're fine," I said with my head tilted at an unnatural angle to the left. I groped to find the connecting button that was yanking the hair off my head. "Thanks anyway," I added cheerfully.

He didn't believe me. "Are you caught?"

"Yes!" Jill confessed the obvious. "Can you see from up there where my shirt is caught on the tree?"

He gingerly came toward us.

I didn't blame him for his caution. Why would two women be wedged under a tree root, appearing to be joined at the hip, with Jill's right arm suspended in midair and my oddly twisted head connected to her wrist? I'm sure we looked like freak show contestants who never made it to the big time and were forced to practice their talents for the unappreciative woodland creatures.

"I can see where it's caught," he said. "It's along the edge. If you can back up a few inches, it should come off on its own. In theory."

I could smell his sweat as he got closer, and for some reason the unpleasant odor was more of an irritant to me at the moment than our predicament.

"I think I can back up." Jill crouched and pulled her arm down. Consequently, my hair and twisted head went down with her.

"Ouch!"

"Sorry!"

"A little more to the left," the jogger said.

"Got it." Jill raised herself and moved forward untangled.

"Oww!"

"Kathy, I'm so sorry. Hold still. I can see where you're caught. There, got it."

Crawling all the way out of our hobbit hideout, we stood up straight and smoothed our hair and crumpled clothes. Then, as if we had practiced, we simultaneously brushed off our behinds with the same synchronized motions and turned to our jogger hero with what I'm sure must have looked like clown grins.

He sized up the situation. "All right then. Looks like you're clear. I'll be on my way. Cheers."

We stood in place, watching him jog on down the trail.

"I wonder which one of us he thinks is Lucy and which one is Ethel," Jill said.

I didn't catch on to her joke at first, but as soon as the *I Love Lucy* connection hit me, I snickered. "You can be Lucy."

"I think I was the Ethel in this caper because I let you talk me into crawling under that tree. You were the Lucy."

"I promise I'll never ask you to do that again."

"Yeah, right, Lucy. We'll see about that. You may not be able to talk me into crawling under tree roots again, but I have a feeling you'll come up with a few more stunts before this sitcom ends in three months."

"Three months?"

"When you go back to California."

The thought that popped into my mind was, *I don't want to leave.* I was astounded to realize I had experienced a mental turnaround from twenty-four hours ago, when I was making another big *X* on the calendar inside my checkbook register. That *X* represented the checking off of another day of exile in New Zealand. Today I wanted a big eraser so I could go back and capture every day of the two weeks I'd lost wallowing in self-pity. What a difference a day makes. What a difference a friend makes.

"How about some lunch?" Jill asked once we had shaken ourselves off and gotten back in the car.

We stopped at a deli and ordered turkey sandwiches to "take away" instead of "to go." The woman behind the register asked if we wanted a bag of *crisps* to go with our *sarnies.*

I turned to Jill for a translation. "Potato chips," she whispered. "To go with our sandwiches."

"Oh, no thanks."

I tried to pay, but Jill insisted I put my wallet back. "You can get the hokey pokey later."

"The hokey pokey? Does that involve putting my right foot in or my left foot out? Because I think we should coordinate our movements ahead of time, so we don't get stuck anywhere. I mean, not that something like that would ever happen to us."

The woman at the register was not amused, but Jill was.

"Hokey pokey is ice cream," Jill explained. "It's nice and creamy with bits of honey nougats in it."

"Ice cream? Why didn't you say so? In that case, I'll gladly buy."

We took our sandwiches to the car, and as we drove back to Jill's house to eat, I thought of how quickly I had come to feel the ebb and flow of friendship with Jill. In California I'd had the same friends for years. We formed a small circle and gathered regularly at church and school events. A few of us got together for lunch to celebrate our birthdays. We were close and comfortable and always there for each other.

With Jill I felt that same connectedness, even though we only had been doing life together for a few days. It felt luxurious to slip so quickly into the coziness of friendship.

Jill pulled up to a stop sign, and we waited for two older women to toddle across the street. They wore sensible shoes and matching hand-knit caps and scarves, and walked with their arms linked. The slow-moving women reached the other side of the street, where they turned together and waved at Jill and me with appreciative smiles. We waved back.

The world seemed to be full of friends.

No matter where a woman is, she can always find a pal.

Rolling through the intersection, we drove a few more blocks before turning up an inclined driveway. "Welcome to my humble abode," Jill said.

I expected a cottage-style home like Mr. Barry's, but Jill's house was closer to the water and looked like a beach house built in the sixties along the cliffs in Laguna. It had a raised front deck that was beautifully decorated with potted plants and sturdy metal lawn furniture. A canvas umbrella was opened over the glass-topped table, and sitting on the table, surrounding the umbrella's pole, was an elaborate metal candleholder with at least six loops. At the end of each loop was a votive candle in a glass holder. I could image how magical the candles must look when lit at night with the lights of the homes across the bay easily visible from the deck.

I noticed right away that all the flowers in Jill's planters were red, white, and blue with a few dashes of yellow added. At my home in Tustin, I used red, white, and blue flowers also.

We also had the same taste in furniture and decorations. Jill's home was done in neutrals. She had cream-colored walls, cocoa brown furniture, deep brown wooden table and chairs, and all her appliances were black. Majestic purple and shimmering, soft gold were the colors that accented her neutral foundation.

I never would have selected those two colors, but they were gorgeous. My accents were in blues and yellows. Somehow taking those shades several steps deeper to purple and gold made all the difference between zippy exuberance and quiet elegance.

"I love your house," I said, peering around the open living area and kitchen-dining area.

"Thank you. Ray insisted we buy it when we first got here. I thought we should rent and play it safe in case the job didn't work out for him, but he said the market value was going to skyrocket, and he was right. We bought this for a song, compared to California prices. The house was twenty-four years old when we bought it, so we had to make a lot of repairs. That turned out to be a bonus because it gave us a chance to change things to the way we liked them."

"You have a gorgeous home," I said. "So many beautiful paintings!"

"I taught an art appreciation class in California for nine years. When we moved here, I taught the same class at Victoria University for three years, but then they hired a full-time teacher."

"Did you paint any of these?"

"No, I only appreciate them. Would you like something to drink?"

"Sure. Whatever you have, I'll have the same."

"Is Fresh Up okay?"

"Sure. I've never had it before, but I'm willing to try it."

"It's juice. Nothing fancy. This one is apple-mango."

"Sounds good."

As I was following Jill into her kitchen, I stopped in front of a black-and-white photo hanging on the wall. I felt entranced by the beauty of the composition.

The picture was a close-up of an infant sleeping, balanced on the broad forearm of a tender father. The infant's head was cupped in the father's open hand, which was huge in comparison to the newborn yet so gently covering, protecting, blessing the tiny, naked miracle.

"This is amazing," I said in a low voice.

Jill joined me with two tall glasses of Fresh Up in her hands and looked lovingly at the picture. "That's my son. He's holding their firstborn. My first grandbaby. Lacey."

"She's beautiful! And this photo is so beautifully done. Who took the picture?"

"My son's mother-in-law. Our little Lacey-girl was only two days old."

I looked at the signature in the corner to see if I recognized the photographer's name. "Laurinda Sue?"

"Yes. She's amazing. Her work is really taking off. It's wonderful because her husband is a painter, and for years his work got all the attention. I guess the story goes that she was taking photographs for years but never showed them to anyone. I'm not sure what brought her work out of the drawer, but she's won a few awards, and one of her pieces is on display at a large hotel in Hawaii."

"Laurinda Sue," I repeated, certain I hadn't heard of her. "You said she's married to a painter?"

Jill hesitated, as if measuring if she could trust me with information that appeared to be a family secret. "She's married to Gabriel Giordani."

My mouth dropped open. "Your son married into the Giordani family?"

She nodded.

Gabriel Giordani's work was everywhere in the U.S. He was known as "The Painter of Hideaways" and had been popular for well over a decade. I owned a box of greeting cards with pictures of cottages he had painted. My mom had a print of one of his garden scenes over her fireplace.

"This is really extraordinary," I murmured, trying not to say anything ridiculous about the Giordani connection. Just in and of itself, the composition of the photograph was exceptional. It didn't need a Giordani endorsement.

"I love this picture," Jill said in a wistful voice. "Not just because it's of my son and my grandbaby, but whenever I look at it, I get a sense of comfort. I think it's because that's how I picture God holding me these past few years. I'm the fragile infant, and He's the strong, Almighty Protector who has held me in the palm of His hand."

Jill's words caused my throat to swell and my eyes to brim with tears. I had no response. I, too, was an infant, more aware than I'd ever been that God wasn't just looking down from His heavenly throne, the all-powerful judge evaluating all of my actions. He cared for me with such gentle mercy that He wouldn't allow me to fall out of my empty nest and tumble headlong into self-destruction. He caught me and held me securely in the palm of His hand.

Seven

Two days after Jill and I made our on-line travel plans for Christchurch, it rained buckets. For the first time since we had arrived in New Zealand, I reached for a small devotional book one of my friends had given me as a going-away gift. The reading for that day was from Ephesians 5.

One verse stood out to me, and I underlined it. "Mostly what God does is love you. Keep company with him and learn a life of love. Observe how Christ loved us. His love was not cautious but extravagant. He didn't love in order to get something from us but to give everything of himself to us. Love like that."

For a long time I sat listening to the rain hitting the garage's metal roof, sounding like rubber pellets. I didn't know if I had ever loved anyone extravagantly, the way God loved me. Finding Jill certainly had been an extravagant gift to me from God. I thought of all the people I had loved cautiously over the years. *What would my life look like if I started to love extravagantly?*

The next morning the sun was back, Tony was out the door early, and I was ready to trot down to the Chocolate Fish for a morning wake-up mocha.

I found Mr. Barry already out in his garden. He greeted me with a wave of his gloved hand from where he kneeled beside the mums. He was trying to tie up the drooping stems. I waved back and thought how he seemed the sort of man who, by virtue of his build, was better suited for shouldering a plow and driving a team of oxen than bending low to fiddle with tying delicate knots in gardening twine.

"How are you this morning, Mr. Barry?"

"No complaints."

I noticed that Mr. Frodo was looking his cheerful self. I also noticed that the blooms on the mums had become so heavy in the rain that they bent in such a way that their golden faces appeared to kiss the earth.

Deciding that I better come clean as well, I bent my head and said, "Mr. Barry, I didn't tell you this yet, but a few days ago I was driving a truck, and I bumped into your lawn hobbit. He fell over, but we put him back up. I broke off a few flowers, but that was all. I don't think anything in your garden was hurt, but I thought I should tell you."

"I saw the whole thing," he said.

"You did?"

"The three of you were a box of budgies."

I wasn't sure what that meant, but I guessed it was something positive by the way he said it. "So you're not upset?"

"How could I be? Best entertainment I've had in a year."

Relieved and yet still feeling a bit penitent, I asked, "Do you need some help?"

He hesitated before nodding and moved back so I could get in there and bolster up the drooping blossoms.

"My wife planted these six years ago. Every year her chrysanthemums keep coming back."

I assumed Mr. Barry's wife had passed away. After going through all the emotions with Jill when she told me about Ray, I wasn't sure I wanted to open up any repressed feelings in this gentle giant. Instead, I nodded to the gunnysack marked Narcissus Bulbs. "Do you plan to put those in the garden today?"

"Thought I would. Might be nice to have some flowers here in October."

"I'd be glad to help, if you like." I knew my gesture wasn't exactly extravagant, but it was a first step toward loving someone without being cautious or thinking about what I could ask for in return.

"I don't mind if you don't mind," Mr. Barry said.

I picked up a trowel and asked where he wanted the first bulb to go. The rain during the past two days had made the earth nice and soft. Getting my hands into fresh, moist soil met some sort of basic need inside me. I felt happy the moment my fingers curled around the rich earth.

Mr. Barry asked if I wanted gloves, but I was enjoying the feel of the soil and told him I didn't have fancy fingernails that were in danger of breaking off.

"My wife used to paint her fingernails red. Bright red. She painted them every week. I liked her red fingernails. You could always see her hands moving about. Even from across the room."

"Did she paint her toenails, too?"

"No, she's always hated her feet. Hates her ears, too. Never wanted to wear her hair back like yours is now. Said she was afraid people would stare at her ears. Why are women like that? Dorothea has beautiful ears."

I noticed he was talking about his wife as if she were alive. I risked broaching a volatile topic and said, "I'd like to hear more about your wife."

"She doesn't say much, but she gets by."

I wasn't sure what that meant.

"She'd like to meet you."

"Okay. Would this morning be a good time?"

"Good as any."

Sliding the last few bulbs into the cool earth, I rose, dusted off my knees, and followed Mr. Barry into the celery-colored cottage to meet Dorothea. She was seated by the window in a wheelchair with a crooked expression on her face. When she saw me, her eyes brightened.

I went to her, slipped my hand in her quavering left hand, and introduced myself.

Dorothea made a soft sound in the back of her throat and kept looking at me. The fingers on her right hand were curled in, and her wrist was bent. I recognized all the symptoms. My grandfather had a stroke when I was young and lived with us a full ten years. The stroke incapacitated him on the right side and severely affected his speech, but his mind was all there. Was that the case with Dorothea?

I told her about my husband and what he did at Jackamond Studios. She took in every word, using her expressive eyes to respond.

Mr. Barry offered me a chair. I sat beside Dorothea, still holding her hand. Then I treated her to the delicacy my grandfather always wanted: I gave her news about what was going on in the outside.

First I told her about the bulbs we'd planted and how large the mums were growing. Then I told her about the views Jill and I enjoyed from the top of Mount Victoria. Dorothea's eyes didn't turn away from me even for a moment. She was a medium-framed woman with short white hair that poofed up on her head like a squiggly shower cap. I thought she had very dainty ears, but I didn't mention them. I didn't want her to think her hubby had been telling me secrets about her in the garden.

Clearly, Mr. Barry could help Dorothea in and out of her wheelchair and take care of all her basic needs. But no man can minister to a woman the way another woman can. I wondered if Dorothea had a regular stream of visitors. Even if she did, after spending an hour with her that morning, I decided that for the rest of our stay in Wellington, I'd be one of her regular visitors.

"I'm going to go," I said when her eyes began to droop. I guessed she probably napped a lot. "I don't want to wear out my welcome, but I'll come back and visit you in a few days. Okay?"

She made a gurgling sound in response.

"Good. I'll see you in a few days then."

Mr. Barry walked me out the front door. He cleared his throat awkwardly once we were where Dorothea couldn't hear us. "I'm in your debt," he said in a deep, yet faint voice.

"No, you're not. Tony and I are in your debt. As a matter of fact, Tony wanted me to be sure and pay our rent before next Tuesday. I'm going to be gone for a few days, and we didn't want to be late with the payment."

"All right." He raised his hand to wave as I took off down the street.

The sun was nearly halfway through its paces, but I was still a woman on a mission for a morning mocha. Some things, like a Chocolate Fish mocha latte, I didn't forget about regardless of how many pleasant interruptions blocked my way.

In the week that followed, Jill and I shopped for a new bedspread for me, comfortable travel shoes for her, and something extra special for Dorothea.

Jill came over the morning before we left for Christchurch and helped me give Dorothea my little going-away-for-a-few-days gift. I'd been over to the house to see her nearly every day. My topics of conversation had dwindled by the third visit, so I brought a novel with me the next time. She seemed to love being read to. Especially because the novel I was reading didn't seem the sort of book Mr. Barry might read to her.

When Jill and I entered, Dorothea was waiting for us. "Good morning!" I said. "I brought my friend Jill with me. Jill, this is Dorothea."

Their connection moment was tender but a little awkward. Jill didn't seem to quite know how or where to touch Dorothea. I'd seen visitors act that way with stroke victims before. My grandfather's friends would look at him as if part of him was broken, and they were afraid to touch any other part of him in case that area might break as well.

I slipped my hand in Dorothea's strong left hand and leaned close to press my cheek against hers. "Jill and I have a little surprise for you today."

Dorothea's eyebrows went up as I held out a small gift bag. I looked over my shoulder. Mr. Barry couldn't be seen, but I guessed he was in the kitchen, his usual place of retreat whenever I came to visit. He seemed to want to hear everything but not let me know he was interested in the novel or what I had to chat about.

"Are you ready for this?" I leaned closer and whispered, "Your husband let me know what color you liked. Or at least what color he liked on you."

I pulled a bottle of bright red nail polish from the bag along with a file, a top coat, and some cotton balls.

"What do you think, Dorothea? Would it be okay if Jill and I put a little color on your fingernails?"

The dear woman began to cry.

"Oops!" I said. "I forgot the tissues."

"I have some." Jill reached into her purse.

We pulled up chairs and positioned ourselves. Jill took Dorothea's flexible left hand. I knew how to handle the right one even though it was locked in a curled-up position.

"Let me know if this is uncomfortable in any way." I massaged the palm of her hand.

"Did Kathy tell you that she and I are leaving in the morning for Christchurch?" Jill asked, warming up to the situation once she started to file Dorothea's neglected thumbnail.

"Have you ever been to Christchurch?" I asked.

Dorothea made a response, but it was hard to tell if it was a yes or a no. I half expected Mr. Barry to answer for her from the kitchen, but when he didn't, Jill and I went on as if her contribution to the conversation had been clear.

"We're flying down and taking the train back," Jill said.

"And staying at a bed-and-breakfast. Jill found this place, and it sounds charming. Actually, all of Christchurch sounds lovely. We've heard that the leaves should be gorgeous."

Dorothea made a sound in her throat, and I said, "Do you want me to bring back some big autumn leaves?"

"Aaah."

I let her know I'd bring back a big bouquet of leaves and lots of stories from our trip.

Cheerfully working together, Jill and I lit up Dorothea's smooth fingernails. The red looked even brighter on her nails than it had in the bottle.

"Mr. Barry is going to love this," I whispered. "He'll notice these little holly berries from across the room and think it's already Christmas."

Dorothea's visceral laugh startled Jill, but I'd come to love it. It sounded like a thinner version of Mad Dog's guffaw. I enjoyed those rare puffs from her sunken chest as much as I enjoyed getting a little chocolate fish. It was like receiving a tiny reward for making Dorothea happy.

The manicure was a grand success. When Jill and I left, Dorothea couldn't stop waving at us with her left hand, as if she were the Queen Mum and we were her adoring subjects, which we definitely were.

"Poor Mr. Barry," I said with a giggle, as we crossed the yard back to the garage.

"Why do you say that?" Jill looked at me as if I were being mean.

"There'll be no living with the woman now that she has red nails! Did you see the way she was waving at us? That red-tipped hand will be ordering him all over the place. All she has to do is point, and the man will be powerless to deny her request. Yes, I'd say our work is done here for the day."

Jill smiled. "Wellington was running a little short on super-heroes before you arrived."

"The dynamic duo, that's us. And the dynamic duo has struck again! Armed with only a bottle of nail polish, Lucy and Ethel go where no man wants to go! With a few vibrant strokes we keep up the never-ending battle of finding ways to empower women everywhere!"

We enjoyed a good giggle in front of the hobbit. I thought the fellow should be happy. This was one of the few times the laughs weren't about him.

"What time should I be ready in the morning?" I asked, as Jill and I wound down and were about to go our separate ways to pack.

"Is seven okay? Our flight is at nine, but I like to be early."

"Me, too. And Tony wanted me to thank you again for letting him borrow your car while we're gone."

"No problem. Anytime. I'll see you in the morning." She gave me a hug. "You did a good thing today, Kathy. With Mrs. Barry. That was a good thing."

I basked in the glow of Jill's praise for a little while after she left. What Jill didn't know was that I hadn't really gone out of my way or done anything extraordinary with Mrs. Barry. I did what came naturally and comfortably to me, because I worked with elderly people every day. Jill never had asked about my job, and I hadn't told her. The topic had never come up.

I pulled out my suitcase from under the bed and wondered what conversational topics would come up on our trip to Christchurch. Jill hadn't told me exactly how Ray had passed away, and I didn't feel as if that story was one I wanted to ask for. If she wanted to give it to me one day, I would receive it, but I wouldn't ask.

When we were on the plane together the next morning, I thought Jill was about to give me the story of Ray's death. She mentioned that the studio had an office in Christchurch and how one of the other location managers had been on site in Christchurch the day of the accident.

But that was all she said. So Ray's death had been an accident. She seemed to be fighting against a wave of sadness after giving me that snippet of information, and I didn't want to start down a conversational trail that would set a somber tone for our getaway.

The Christchurch airport was a small building with a single conveyor belt for the luggage. It took us no time to retrieve our suitcases and head outside into the sunny day.

Climbing into the first cab that was waiting at the curb, Jill told the driver the name of our hotel. The cab appeared to be a family van that doubled as a cab. Delicate, white lace doilies covered the headrests.

"These are pretty," Jill said.

"Some of my wife's handiwork," said the driver.

He was a bald man dressed in a long-sleeved white shirt and a red and green plaid vest, and he welcomed us to his hometown by telling us a variety of details about the surrounding area. He had to be at least in his seventies. His grandfather, he said, had come from England and helped settle this province.

"You'll find my city to be the most English city outside of England. That's what I tell everyone who comes here. They all agree with me. You will, too."

"I'm sure we will," Jill said.

"What do you recommend we do while we're here?" I asked.

"It's a nice time of year to go punting. On the Avon. You can hire out a man, and he'll take you. Don't know that they'd let two young ladies such as yourselves hire out a skiff on your own."

His accent was tricky to understand, but I guessed he was talking about going on a boat on the Avon River so I said, "Sounds like fun."

The cab pulled up in front of our bed-and-breakfast, and Jill drew in an appreciative breath. "Look at this house!"

"It looks like the Fontaine Restaurant," I said. "Or I should say, it looks like the house your grandfather built."

"Did you see the front door?" Jill asked after we had paid our driver and started to pull our wheeled suitcases up the front walkway.

"I love the stained glass." I admired the attention to detail on this restored charmer. The walkway was lined with bright yellow marigolds and two large chrysanthemum plants at the bottom of the steps. The mums reminded me of Dorothea.

"Jill, let me get a quick picture of you at the bottom of the steps. I want to show Dorothea the mums."

We took turns posing by the flowers, on the steps, and at the front door next to the stained glass.

"How about one by the railing," I suggested.

"Oh, this porch brings back so many memories," Jill said. "I love this wicker furniture."

"Then let me get some shots of you in the wicker rocking chair."

She chuckled. "You're going to use up all your film in the first five minutes of our trip."

"Don't worry; it's digital," I said. "This is Tony's favorite of our three cameras. I think my limit on this one is five hundred shots, so keep on posing!"

Jill rested her hands on the back of one of the chairs and struck a chin-up, noble-woman-on-a-mild-afternoon pose with a closed-lip, contented expression.

"All you need is a parasol," I told her. "Or a tall glass of lemonade."

"How about this?" Jill reached for a china teacup and saucer resting on the side table. The cup was half full, as if someone had stepped away and might be returning for the final three sips.

"It's still warm!" She held the saucer in the palm of her hand and pretended to take a sip. "I feel like Goldilocks. You better take the picture quick before the three bears return."

The front door opened tentatively. Instead of a bear of any sort, a fair-haired woman in a billowy white blouse looked at us shyly. "Hallo?"

Jill was not the only Goldilocks in this fairy-tale setting.

"Hi." Jill laughed nervously and quickly returned the teacup to where she had found it. "We have reservations. The name is Radovich. We were just enjoying your beautiful porch."

"Thank you," our more relaxed hostess said. "Please come in."

We stepped onto polished dark wood floors and listened as she explained with a hint of a British accent where the *loo* was located down the hall.

"You are both invited to enjoy the front porch, of course, and feel free to make use of the front parlor and breakfast room anytime you wish."

We were shown to our room at the front of the house. The high ceiling was accented by a charming chandelier made from a lacy parasol hung so that the open part served as the shade.

"I love this light." Jill gazed up at the parasol. "I'd like to hang a parasol like this in my bedroom."

"I saw the idea in a magazine," our hostess said. "I still have the magazine. You're welcome to take it with you, if you like."

"Thank you. Yes, I'd love to see how to hang a light like this."

From the tall windows flowed sheer ivory curtains. The twin beds were separated by a gorgeous white table where an amber glass vase exploded with purple asters. On the dresser was an electric pot for heating water and an assortment of tea bags along with a china teapot and two matching china cups and saucers. Next to the teacups a plate of fancy chocolate truffles waited for us.

"This is charming," Jill said. "Everything about your home is beautiful."

"Thank you." Our hostess gave a humble bow, as she left us to settle in.

"Does it remind you a lot of the house you grew up in?" I tried out the bed closest to the window.

"Only from the outside. Everything inside is different—the floor plan, the ceilings, the staircase. But I love it, don't you?"

"I do. Especially our room. It feels as if we stepped into a party that's all set up and waiting for us."

"It does! So what are we waiting for? Let's start to party!" Jill lifted the plate of goodies and graciously offered me first choice of the chocolates.

If I hadn't already decided that I liked Jill as much as I did, that one gesture of offering me first choice of the chocolates would have cinched our friendship forever.

Eight

S o, *what should we do first?"* I was leisurely enjoying the last drop of tea from one of the china cups that had been waiting for Jill and me in our lovely B&B bedroom in Christchurch. The chocolate lifted our adventurous spirits, and we were ready to take on the town.

"We should find a map first," Jill suggested.

"I saw a rack of brochures in the front room when we came in. I'm sure a map would be there. I'll go see what they have."

"How about if I meet you in the front room in a minute? I'm going to change. It's a lot warmer here than I thought it would be."

I left Jill and browsed through the rack of travel brochures. The first brochure I pulled out gave information about one of the visitor centers that offered cultural presentations by the Maori.

On the back of the brochure the words, "*Ki mai koe ki a au,*

93

he aha te mea nui tenei ao," appeared over a photo of a Maori warrior complete with a tattooed face, frighteningly popped-out eyes, and an open mouth in a roaring expression.

Under that photo was a picture of a Maori man greeting another by coming nose to nose in a warm expression of friendship. The words under that photo were, "*He tangata, he tangata, he tangata.*"

"Are you thinking of going to Rotorua?" a voice behind me asked.

I jumped. I hadn't seen the man sitting in a side chair when I entered the front room. His dark, kinky hair looked how Mad Dog's might look, if he ever got it cut.

"I'm not sure. It looks fascinating."

"That's because we're a fascinating people." He grinned. Then he rose and came toward me with a book in his hand. "I'm Hika."

I introduced myself and explained that I was visiting.

"I live here." He grinned again, as if he knew a secret I wasn't in on.

I assumed he was renting a room. "It's a charming place, isn't it?"

Instead of agreeing with me, he thanked me for the compliment and said, "My wife and I bought this house five years ago. It was her dream to run an inn after I retired. Here's the picture of what it looked like when we started the project." He pointed to a framed picture on the wall.

"Wow! What a transformation."

"Thank you."

"That's a nice portrait." I pointed to a pencil sketch of an aging Maori man's profile. Over his shoulders he wore a cape of some sort.

"My grandfather," Hika said. "He was a Maori chief. I'm named after him."

"Really? My great-grandfather was a chief also. He was Navajo."

Hika's expression sobered. He tilted his head in reverent acknowledgment. It was as if he were honoring me as a descendant of a chief. I didn't quite know how to respond. That bit of lineage trivia had rarely prompted a response of respect in the past.

"And you?" I asked cautiously. I didn't want to say the wrong thing and have him stick out his tongue or pop out his eyes like the warrior on the back of the brochure, but I wanted to honor his heritage as well. "Have you always lived in this area?"

"No, I'm from the North Island. From Auckland." He said a few words that I couldn't understand, and I supposed them to be the name of his tribe. I didn't know how to ask further, because I didn't know if the Maoris were from tribes or clans or what.

"I know very little about Maoris," I admitted, holding up the brochure in my hand. "Maybe I should go to this cultural center."

"It's on the North Island. It will take you a day to get there." With a hint of mischief in his expression he added, "Since you are staying here for two nights, I don't think you should check out early to make the journey. We don't like it when our guests leave early."

"Don't worry; we're planning to stay both nights."

"Good. Now, if you want to know about Maori culture, I can tell you a few things. And what I don't know I can make up."

I smiled and lowered myself onto a chair in the parlor.

Hika took the chair across from me and told me how the Polynesian Maoris had paddled their way through the South Pacific in huge, elaborately decorated, dugout sailing canoes before settling in New Zealand at least a thousand years ago. Dutch sailors were the first Europeans to make contact with the Maori in the late 1600s. But four of the sailors were clubbed to death, and so the captain sailed on without exploring any more of New Zealand.

"A hundred years later Captain Cook and his crew showed up, and none of the sailors were killed this time. That was good for them, but it was not good for us, because the explorers left two things behind we did not need: guns and measles. More Europeans came bringing more civilization and more means of death. But then, I am telling you a story that is familiar to you."

"No. As I said, I don't know anything about the Maoris."

"I was referring to the story of the Native Americans."

I wasn't prepared to feel as sad as I did at the impact of his words. "Western civilization hasn't been good for indigenous people during the past three hundred years, has it?"

Hika pointed to the italicized words on the back of the brochure I was holding and repeated them in a deep voice. "*Ki mai koe ki a au, he aha te mea nui tenei ao.*"

"What does that mean?"

"It is the first part of the proverb. A question. 'If you should ask me what is the most important thing in the world, the answer would be…?'"

He waited a moment for me to respond. If I were in the middle of a Bible study group or a circle of friends from my church, I would know the expected answer. Jesus had made it clear that the greatest commandment was to love the Lord your

God with all your heart, soul, strength, and mind. I didn't know what answer Hika would expect here in this place of upside down. My guess was something like land or tribal rights, or freedom.

When I didn't jump in with a response, Hika said, "The answer is, '*He tangata, he tangata, he tangata.*'"

"And what does that mean?"

"'It's the people, it's the people, it's the people.'"

Hika sat back, waiting for the proverb to sink in. It struck me that this was the second part of the great commandment Jesus gave to His disciples: love your neighbor as yourself.

That's it. Love God and love people. Not one or the other. It's both.

I thought about the extravagant love verse in Ephesians and how the passage said to "learn a life of love." Loving God and loving people don't come naturally to any of us. We all have to be taught to value others and to learn a life of love.

Just then Jill entered the parlor and apologized for taking so long. I made the introductions, and Jill asked if I'd found a map yet. She asked how we could rent a boat to take down the Avon River.

Hika rose, reached for another brochure, and handed it to me. This one was of Christchurch with a clear map on the back.

"Thanks. I appreciate the information. Not only the map but also everything you said. Thank you."

Jill and I stepped out onto the porch. We were equipped with everything we needed for our journey into the fresh autumn afternoon. Meandering down the charming streets of Christchurch, we followed the map to the river Avon.

I thought of how different everything had been for me a

few short weeks ago when I was sitting around in sweats or pj's all day, closed up in the garage apartment. If someone had asked me then if I loved God, I would have said yes, of course. I never stopped loving God just because life had taken such a flip.

But I was in hiding. I wasn't around people, people, people.

Meeting Jill, kneeling beside Mr. Barry in the garden, holding Dorothea's hand—these were the treasures of this place. Being in the midst of people was what brought life back to me.

Jill and I continued along the twisting river trail. Well-watered trees rose above us and shaded our path. One after another of the gentle giants stood guard on their thick trunks and stretched out long strings of quivering leaves that they dangled over our heads. Every time the wind blew, a few more glittering gold coin leaves showered over us and tumbled down to the green earth. I selected a collection of them for Dorothea.

"I feel like I'm in Narnia," Jill said.

"I know. This is a fabulous place, isn't it?"

"You know what's amazing to me?" Jill stopped to snap a picture. "Do you remember my saying that Christchurch is the launching point for journeys to Antarctica, because this is the closest major city to the bottom of the world?"

"Yes, I remember your saying that."

"Well, you would think that for being so close to all that ice and all those penguins it would be much colder here. This is a place of surprises."

I agreed with her as we strolled past a large arch labeled the "Bridge of Remembrance." The inscription commemorated the gunners from that region who had served in World Wars I and II.

"Have you noticed a lot of war memorials since you've been in New Zealand?" Jill asked.

"Not particularly."

"You'll probably start to notice them now. If I remember correctly, over one hundred thousand troops from New Zealand fought in World War I, and over half of the soldiers were killed or wounded. For a small nation, it was devastating. Everyone knew someone who lost someone. I think it affected that entire generation in a deep way."

"I never thought of New Zealanders being involved in either of the world wars."

"That's because you and I grew up only hearing about America's part in fighting for world peace during the past century. It's a little stunning, isn't it, when you slip into a place like this and realize that we're not really the center of the universe after all?"

I stopped walking along the river trail and looked at Jill.

"Are you okay?"

"What you just said got to me. It's true. We're not the center of the universe, are we?"

"Certainly not the way we think we are."

I felt as if all kinds of new ideas were coming at me today. Jill's and Hika's comments weren't earthshaking, but they prompted me to think beyond myself. Both of them presented thoughts that were larger than the small, familiar world I'd lived in for so long. I decided I liked being shaken out of my comfort zone every now and then.

We picked up the pace and found the Antigua Boat Sheds without any trouble. Next to the rental stall was a waterfront café. The handwritten sign on the front offered pumpkin basil soup with bacon as the special of the day.

"What do you think? Should we eat first?" Jill asked.

I didn't have to be invited twice to try the local special of the day. We slid onto the bench of a picnic table on the patio and watched dozens of ducks as they paddled up to the riverbank's edge. They looked up to us, waiting for a snack to be sent their way. Once Jill's sandwich was served, she shared more than half her bread with them. We laughed as their bobbing white tails wiggled every time they ducked under for the next bite.

Several refined swans arrived, turning their long necks to gaze up at us. Their elegant forms alongside the pale pink roses that had climbed over the wall and lined the railing between us and the water set the perfect fairy-tale scene. The river was as blue as the sky and was all lit up with the sparkling reflection of diamond-cut sunshine. I couldn't wait to get in a canoe and paddle along with the ducks and swans.

A cocky young man at the boat rental stall greeted us with a tip of his straw hat. He seemed to think it humorous that the two of us "older" women wanted to rent a canoe and take it out by ourselves. He tried to convince us to wait half an hour until Evan, the boatman, returned with the fancy flatboat that most tourists "our age" preferred to take. Evan was, after all, an excellent punter.

Jill and I exchanged glances, and I knew we were of one mind.

"No thank you," we both said.

"We'd prefer to take out a canoe on our own," Jill added.

"All right then. You can have the red one there at the dock."

We paid with cash, picked up our paddles and life vests, and clambered into the canoe while the young man at the boat stall watched.

Not being particularly experienced at canoeing, Jill and I got in facing each other instead of both facing the same direction.

"That's not the way you should be seated," the young man said with a snicker.

"This is the way we seat," I said.

"Seat?"

"Sit," I declared, settling in with as much dignity as I could at that point. "This is the way we sit."

Jill was no help. She was laughing, and that made me want to laugh. But the situation wasn't as funny as she may have thought because the challenge of swinging my legs around without unbalancing the canoe was more of a risk than I was willing to take.

"Do you want to turn the other way?" I asked Jill quietly.

"No, we can make this work. Come on, I'll paddle us out of here."

I am happy to report that we pulled off the procedure as graceful as swans and floated with the current into the center of the shallow river.

But once we moved away from the dock, our challenges came to the forefront. That's when I put my paddle in the water, and Jill and I couldn't synchronize our paddling. Every stroke I made seemed to cancel hers.

"Right side," Jill called out.

I paddled vigorously.

"Your other right side!" she said, laughing. "We're headed for the tules!"

I never was good at determining my right from my left when in a pinch. With four bold strokes, I managed to ram us right into the tall grasses along the riverbank.

"Let me try to back us up," Jill said. "Don't paddle."

I realized then that the current was more of a problem than we had anticipated. In the deeper water toward the center of the river, the current appeared to gently flow back toward the boathouse. Along the side, where we were now wedged, a different, swirling current was at play.

Jill single-handedly maneuvered us out of the reeds and back into the calmer current, which, unfortunately, carried us right back to the dock at the boathouse before she and I had a chance to regroup and coordinate our paddling efforts.

"Hallo!" the smarty boat-boy greeted us from the launching dock where he had no doubt seen our entire escapade. "Does this mean we can sign you up then for the punting tour?"

"Just ignore him," Jill said under her breath, as if we were two girls at summer camp and the older boys from the neighboring camp had invaded our lake.

I thought she was hilarious to say we should ignore him, but I couldn't do it. I had to smart off. After all, he was wearing a straw hat and a bow tie like a missing member of a barbershop quartet. He was begging for sassy comments from the tourists.

"We're not sissies in this scenario."

"That's right. We are managing just fine, thank you," Jill added politely.

"Yeah. Save your punting tickets for some other old ladies."

"Kathy!" Jill flipped a sprinkling of water on me with her paddle. "Who are you calling an old lady?"

"Not us!"

"Exactly," she agreed. "Not us."

We managed to paddle from the boathouse and successfully move up the lazy river. The secret was for me to paddle

backwards from how Jill was paddling, as well as on the opposite side. Somehow this procedure seemed fitting in light of
everything else that felt upside down and backwards in this
place.

The farther we paddled up the river, the more peaceful and
shadowed the river became. On both sides of the water were
long stretches of green grass with trees, benches, and concrete
bike trails. Women pushing baby strollers smiled at us. Little
children waved at us. A man on a bike took such a long look at
our unorthodox seating position and paddling that his front
tire went off the trail. He wobbled himself back on course and
kept going, still casting glances at us over his shoulder.

"It's nice to have all the boys around here looking at us,
isn't it?" Jill asked with a giggle. It seemed to me she was feeling
the lightness of being adorable for the first time in a long time.

I considered reminding her why all the boys were paying
attention to us middle-aged mamas. We weren't a couple of
cute, young cheerleaders; we were inexperienced tourists,
demonstrating our strange canoe-maneuvering techniques. I
thought we resembled Dr. Dolittle's pushmi-pullyu creature,
that endearing, two-headed alpaca that was joined in the
middle. But if Jill was feeling young and flirty and having a
great time, I wasn't going to be the one to spoil her fun.

Nine

Our canoe slid underneath a charming arched walking bridge as Jill chattered enthusiastically. "Don't you love the colors on the trees? They are so gorgeous. And that green area on the right must be Hagley Park. I read about it. When the city fathers built Christchurch, they set aside almost a square mile for a public park. A restaurant is at the edge of the herb garden. We might have to include a visit there on our pressing itinerary."

"Oh, yes, our pressing itinerary. I like the way you think. Eat a little, float a little. Eat a little, walk a little. My idea of a true vacation."

The river took a turn and came into a sunny area where more bobbing ducks peeked underwater for treats. They seemed to be on the same schedule as we were: eat a little, quack a little. Eat a little, paddle a little.

Floating toward us was a beautifully painted flatboat with a young man standing in the back, wearing a straw hat, white shirt, and bow tie. He was using a long pole to punt his passengers down the river.

"Look, Jill! It's Evan the punter we heard so much about. Should we wave?"

"We can do better than that." Jill paddled faster. "Come on."

She maneuvered our canoe within six feet of the sedate, "older" tourists who were sitting back with terry cloth hats on their heads and cameras around their necks.

"Hi, Evan," Jill called out.

"Hi, Evan," I echoed.

We were the two most popular girls on the lake at summer camp all over again.

"You're doing a great job, Evan," Jill said coyly.

"You're the best punter on the river, Evan," I added.

The tourists were all looking at us, startled at such enthusiasm in the middle of their placid float.

"Would you sing for us, Evan? Please?" Jill was pushing it now, but I remained her faithful sidekick.

"Yeah, Evan. We love it when you sing."

With one motion all Evan's passengers turned their heads and looked at him. He had gone red faced under his straw hat.

Evan kept punting, ignoring us and our request for a song. With a few significant strokes of the long punting pole, he was out of range from us and heading around a bend.

"Oh, Evan," Jill called after him, "you're breaking my heart!"

"Just one song!" I pleaded in a shout that echoed off the riverbank.

Evan was too far around the bend by then to glare at us. Jill and I leaned toward the center of our canoe and burst into laughter.

"Did you see the look on his face?" Jill said. "It was like his mother had come to check up on him his first day on the job!"

"I know. Poor kid. Too bad we aren't seventeen anymore. I think we could have talked him into taking us to the movies tonight."

"I never would have imagined you to be such a big flirt," Jill said. "You must have had all the guys wrapped around your little finger in high school."

"No, never. I would never have tried to pull a stunt like that in high school."

"I would have." Jill flipped her hair behind her ear.

"I can believe that. It's just one more reason I'm glad you and I met now instead of then."

"It's much more fun being flirty now. Trust me, you saved the best for the second half of life."

With more skill than either of us realized we could manage, we turned our little red convertible around and headed down the Avon River with the current speeding our journey. It seemed a symbol of how my life had been filled with so many years of paddling upstream, and now the current was hastening me forward into the fast-approaching second half of life. I knew I was going to be a different person. I already was.

"Look." Jill giggled.

Evan was waiting for us on the dock.

"Hello," Jill said calmly. All the silliness had subsided.

"I wanted to thank the two of you." Evan reached out a hand to help us from the canoe.

"Why?" Jill asked, as if by playing coy she could deny that we were the sassy canoers at the bend in the river.

"They liked your girly stunt back there."

I hid a smile. Those other "older" women who were punting with Evan were as young at heart as Jill and me. No doubt they wished they had rented the red canoe instead.

"They wouldn't stop badgering me about the song."

"Did you sing for them?" I asked.

"Yes, I did." His wide grin revealed a crooked front tooth and a light heart. "They liked the song so much I was given the most tips I've ever received from a tour group. So thanks. Thanks a lot."

We shook hands with grinning Evan. Generous Jill pulled out some money from her pocket and stuffed it in his hand. "Thanks for being such a good sport."

"No, thank you, really."

"You know what this means, don't you?" I asked. "Those people are going to tell their friends about Evan the Singing Punter, and you are going to get more special requests from tour groups than you can handle."

"All right by me!"

We had left Evan and were back on the river walkway when Jill said with great satisfaction, "The dynamic duo strikes again! We may very well have changed the course of history for all the punters in New Zealand."

"Not to mention setting an example of a stylish new mode for seating oneself in a canoe."

"Our way worked just fine," Jill said. "We didn't tip over or anything."

We topped off the waning afternoon with a little shopping and a lot more walking and followed it up with a wonderful night's sleep at our B&B.

In the morning, Hika and his wife served breakfast in the sunroom, complete with homemade fig jam and scones. We took our time getting out to see what we could see. We were moving at a much more leisurely pace than how things moved when Tony and I traveled together.

The most comfortable part of the trip for me was the way I felt the freedom to be alone with my thoughts when I wanted to. I didn't feel obligated to fill the space between Jill and me with words every moment we were together. That was refreshing, and I was processing a lot.

Jill seemed to be doing the same.

Our first stop was the town square only three blocks away.

"I love this Gothic Revival architecture." Jill stood in front of the cathedral and took it all in. "Don't you?"

I didn't want to tell her, but my eye had wandered from the architecture and was on the familiar coffeehouse logo on a building in the opposite corner of the square. We had been served tea for breakfast, and coffee was sounding pretty good.

"Yes, wonderful architecture," I said halfheartedly. "Are you by any chance interested in a little latte? A mocha, maybe? Or an iced tea?"

"It sounds good, but I'm actually more interested in exploring the insides of this church. Is that okay with you?"

"Yes, of course." I felt frivolous for being more excited about standing in the presence of an American coffee chain store than I was about entering a historical landmark.

Inside, the cathedral was dark and calm. Several people were sitting in the pews, quietly observing or perhaps meditating. The deep black wood of the pews fascinated Jill; she kept running her hand over the smooth corners.

"It says here," Jill whispered, reading to me from the tour book we were handed when we entered, "that the wood is from native trees called matai, and the rocks used to build the cathedral were from local quarries. It's beautiful, isn't it?"

I was beginning to grasp the allure of this old church and agreed with Jill. It was a beautiful place. I followed her to the front pew where we sat quietly together. Jill bowed her head and folded her hands.

"I am so thankful for you," Jill said a moment later, leaning close and whispering to me. "You have brought so much life back into my world, Kathy."

"Jill, I feel the same way. If I hadn't met you, I'd probably still be hiding out in our apartment. I am so thankful for the way you've included me in your life."

We both got a little teary as we exchanged a hug around the neck. Standing together, we slowly walked around the rest of the sanctuary and then climbed the 133 steps to the top of the cathedral. I was thankful for my few trots down to the Chocolate Fish and back during the past weeks. Otherwise, I would have been huffing and puffing much more than I was. At the top we took in an amazing view of the small city and the horizon.

"Look how blue the sky is. What shade would you call that?"

Jill looked and said, "New Zealand autumn. Has it been a while since you've seen a blue sky?"

"You remember how it is in Orange County. Lots of haze and smog. The sky is rarely a clear, deep shade of blue like this."

"There's Hagley Park." Jill pointed to a green area accented by lots of huge trees. "Are you interested in walking back over there? Or does a visit to one of the museums sound good?"

"Either one, as long as we fuel ourselves with a latte." I pointed to the coffee shop in the square that I'd noticed on our way into the cathedral. "Come on, my treat."

Jill was still teasing me the next morning about my affection for what she called "popular coffee." Our train to Picton left at 7:30 AM. That meant we were up at 5:30, packed and waiting outside for our cab ride to the train station before the day had barely opened its eyes.

I had barely opened my eyes as well and was lamenting that if we had the time I'd zoom over to the town square and see about getting us two ventis to "take away."

"I'm sure they have some sort of coffee on the train," Jill assured me. "It won't be popular coffee, but it should help us wake up all the same."

I gave an involuntary shiver in the early morning mist and tried not to think about a double espresso, or better yet, an Americano with half-and-half.

Closing my eyes, I saw a row of dancing paper coffee cups with skinny little arms sticking out above the recyclable brown sleeves. They were dancing to a Ray Charles tune. That's when I knew I was: a) overly tired; b) overly creative when it came to diverting my taste buds; or c) in need of a support group for California Coffee Withdrawal Therapy.

Once we were on the train, I asked about coffee and was told to listen for an announcement about when the tea car would open.

"'Tea car,'" I muttered. "That doesn't sound too promising for coffee."

"You know how they say *tea* here, but it can mean lunch or a snack. I think that's all it means. I'd be surprised if they didn't have coffee."

I settled back, watching the scenery roll by outside the large window. Our train seats faced each other with a table in between us. Jill recorded her thoughts and some doodles in her journal. I started to enjoy the brilliant green foliage; the narrow, twisting streams; and the distant hills. The rolling terrain was dotted with white, woolly sheep and pockets of wildflowers.

As we traveled north, the sun came at us in the train car at such an angle we couldn't see much of anything outside. The light seemed to expand and radiate in a wide burst. I felt as if we were traveling back in time to a place of ancient ferns and simple stone walls.

"What are those called, do you know?" I pointed to a clump of fern plants as we rolled past them.

"Those are *pongas*. The shape of the curly fronds out of the top is called *koru*. You'll see that shape a lot in New Zealand art and designs."

"I have noticed it a lot of places," I said. "And what's the story on the kiwi? Which came first? The bird or the fruit?"

"The bird. Definitely the bird came first. The kiwi birds don't fly. Did you know that?"

"No. I don't know anything about them."

"They're nocturnal and are nearly extinct, because they became such easy prey when settlers came with their domestic animals. The kiwi fruit is from China. The Chinese settlers brought vines to New Zealand that they called Chinese gooseberries. When the fruit did well here, they decided to export it and changed the name to kiwi fruit to identify it with New Zealand rather than China."

We talked about the plight of the poor kiwi bird, and I began to understand why many New Zealanders referred to themselves as Kiwis in a sort of compassionate alignment with their dear bird.

As the train rolled into our first stop, a buttonhole called Rangiora, I said, "I feel sorry for any bird that can't fly."

The next thought that popped in my head was, *Even midlife mama birds?*

My immediate mental answer was, *Especially midlife mama birds.*

It was crazy enough that I was asking myself questions like a Maori proverb, but even worse was that I was answering. Besides, if the thought was supposed to be directed toward me, I was already flying. I was soaring.

A mellow voice came on over the speaker announcing that the tea car was now open for service. Passengers were encouraged to "purchase food, which may then be taken with you back to your allocated seats."

Jill and I chuckled at the lengthy explanation.

"Would you like something?" I asked.

"Sure. I wouldn't mind a cup of tea. With cream."

I walked carefully down the slightly rolling floor toward the tea car and was the first passenger to step up to what looked like an ordinary counter at a deli or coffee shop. A clear case displayed wrapped sandwiches. A wire basket by the register offered individually wrapped oatmeal cookies. Behind the young woman who manned the counter was a large sign listing all the food options and prices. She didn't look as if she was quite awake yet.

I smiled at the not-too-cheery blonde and said, "One coffee with cream and—"

"Milk?" she asked.

"No, coffee."

"Coffee with milk," she corrected me.

"Yes."

"White coffee, then."

"Okay. White coffee. And one tea with cream."

"Devonshire tea?"

"No, just tea."

"Not with scones and cream?"

"Just cream, please."

"Right. The Devonshire cream tea, then. Scone or roll with the Devonshire?"

"No…"

"We only have the breakfast roll," she said.

"Yes, I understand. It's just that, all I want is—"

"I've got it. A breakfast roll and one Devonshire tea."

"No." I could feel the impatience of the waiting passengers behind me.

"And the white coffee," she added.

I leaned forward and patiently said, "I would like one white coffee and just one cup of hot tea."

"Of course it comes hot. We don't expect you to have a personal microwave at your seat."

I had no response to her snappy comment. Was she being funny? Was she insulting me? Was I on a hidden camera somewhere?

When I didn't respond, she punched some buttons on the computerized cash register. "Sixteen fifty, then."

"Sixteen dollars and fifty cents for what?"

"Devonshire tea, breakfast roll, and a white coffee."

At a loss for words, I surrendered and handed over a twenty-dollar bill. Stepping to the side, I heard the next customer order with a New Zealand accent and all the right phrases what he wanted.

Another young girl who was behind the barrier to the tiny onboard kitchen reached around the side and handed me a large paper bag, telling me to hold it steady.

Returning to my allocated seat, I placed the large bag on the table.

"What did you get?" Jill asked.

"I have no idea."

Ten

Jill laughed at my flustered response and opened the paper sack I'd brought back from the tea car. "Let's see what they gave you."

"I was trying to buy a single cup of tea for you, but I think I ended up with an entire tea party."

Coffee and tea were in reinforced paper cups with lids. The package also held two large scones, a container with cream as thick as fresh butter, two squares of butter, four packets of raspberry jam, and a plastic knife. The breakfast roll was a long deli roll sprinkled with sesame seeds and packed with fried egg; round, Canadian-style bacon; sliced, grilled tomatoes; and something that looked like flattened hash browns.

Neither of us had any complaints once we started our small feast. Even the coffee was drinkable.

"Our sugar just started to come in elongated packages like this at Riverview, the retirement community where I work," I said. "It's been so confusing for the residents because they're used to sugar in little rectangular packets."

"What do you do at Riverview? You said it's a retirement community, but what's your position there?"

"It's not very glamorous. My title is assistant, and that's what I do. I assist. Some days I organize group trips to the Bowers Museum or to lunch at Mimi's Café. Other days I change the bulletin boards in all the halls or help Mrs. Swensen carry her laundry basket back to her apartment."

"Or give a manicure every now and then?" Jill asked.

"I've given a few. I like visiting the residents who have been there a long time. Some of them move over to the assisted living section of our campus, and I love it when I go to see them and they remember me."

"What's your favorite part of your job?"

I leaned back and wondered if anyone had ever asked me that. "The hours have always been great. I started part-time when Skyler was in elementary school, and I could always adjust my hours to fit around my family. That was a huge bonus."

"But what do you enjoy the most when you're at work?"

"I don't know."

"Sure you do. Just off the top of your head, what's your favorite part of a workday?"

I said the first thing that came to mind. "I love being with stroke patients when they meet with their speech therapists."

"Why?"

I didn't feel as if Jill was putting me on the spot like a lawyer trying to uncover facts. Instead, she seemed to be turning over the soil of my heart like a tender gardener. She was preparing me for new bulbs that would burrow inside my thoughts and bloom in another season.

"I guess I like being around the speech therapists so much

because I see how they give the patients hope. When you've spent your whole life depending on talking as your way to get your thoughts across, it's horrible to have your voice taken from you."

I was on my soapbox now and sat up straighter. "Most people think the worst part of a stroke is losing the use of an arm or not being able to walk without assistance. What no one understands is how debilitating it is to lose your words. If you can't talk, people ignore you. They don't try to interact with you. Your needs and your opinions go unnoticed and unheeded.

"Whenever a speech therapist breaks through with a patient, that's when I say, 'This has been a good day.' Those are my favorite days. It doesn't mean every patient has the ability to train his throat and mouth to form words again. Some of them learn sign language or learn to write short thoughts on a pad. One therapist designed a special board for Mr. Harris that had big colored dots. Red for no, green for yes, yellow for hungry...it was so great. I loved seeing Mr. Harris's face light up when he discovered he could communicate again."

I paused to take a breath, and with a shrug I added, "I get a little passionate about this, I guess."

Jill grinned. "So, why aren't you a speech therapist?"

"Because I only went to community college for three semesters."

"So?"

"So, it takes a little more education than that to work as a speech therapist."

"So why don't you go back to school?"

"Because..."

I didn't finish the sentence because I didn't have a good reason. I hadn't seriously thought through the option in a long time. So much of my life had been about helping out with Tony's mom while she was still alive and then getting Skyler to college. Tony and I had worked hard to make sure she had the chance to go all the way through college and receive her BA. The past six months I had been focused on working as many extra hours as I could to pay for remodeling the kitchen. I hadn't spent any time thinking about the remodeling I could do in my life.

"I don't know; I don't know why I can't go back to school."

"I think you should," Jill said.

We left the topic out on the table, as the train rolled through a series of tunnels. My thoughts were experiencing the same light sensory changes of rushing through darkness into light and then back into darkness. First light, then dark. Light, dark.

Maybe I could go back to school…No, that's crazy. I can't do it…Yes, I can…No, I can't…Why not?

We rolled through a long tunnel and emerged with the shimmering South Pacific Ocean on the right. The sand that lined the shore was dark as obsidian and littered with kelp. Not a person was in sight.

The train slowed, and we could see from our observation car that we were coming into a town along the dark sand of Kaikoura Peninsula.

"Look!" Jill pointed to the ocean. "Dolphins!"

A dozen of the gray creatures were leaping in the blue water less than a quarter of a mile from the train.

"Wow! Did you see that one jump? It looked like it spun around in the air."

The train came to a stop, and the mellow-voiced conductor let us know we were taking a five-minute respite, in which we were allowed to get off the train and stretch our legs.

"Let's get off," Jill said. "We can take a closer look at those dolphins."

We exited the train, aided by the kind hand of a uniformed railroad assistant. Stepping through the small train station that doubled as a souvenir and snack shop, we walked out onto a broad cement patio. Below us, down the stairs, was the dark sand and pebble beach and beyond the sand were the rolling waves and playful dolphins.

"Look at them!" Jill pointed to the ocean. "They are having so much fun out there."

As the next large wave curled, we could see more dolphins rising in the surf.

"They are so sleek," she said. "I think dolphins are amazing, don't you? Look at how happy they are."

"They are."

Jill turned to me. "Come on! Quick! Let's run through the sand and touch the water."

Suddenly Jill was the land dolphin, dashing down the stairs, ready to play. "I'll race you," she called over her shoulder as soon as her feet hit the sand.

I rushed down the stairs and fiddled with my shoes and socks until my feet were naked.

Just then the train whistle sounded. Our five-minute respite already was over. The train was ready to leave.

Jill was at the water's edge, waving with big arm motions for me to join her. I pointed back at the tracks and yelled, "The train is leaving!"

She motioned again for me to come, her feet playfully kicking a spray of salt water in my direction. In a split second, I made my decision and ran to the water. One of us had to be the designated driver when Jill went into her intoxicating flirt mode. This time she was flirting with nature. I barely touched my toe to the wet sand and hollered over the roar of the surf, "We have to go!"

"Wait! Just look!"

A nearly translucent wave was cresting so close to shore that we could have swum out to meet it, if we were strong enough. In the curl of the wave we saw two dolphins, their noses jutting forward like the balancing arm of a surfer. The dolphins were riding the wave together.

Jill and I turned to each other with expressions of wide-eyed, open-mouthed wonder. We tilted our heads back, shooting our full-hearted laughter into the air the way the care-free dolphins were shooting the curl.

Over the blend of joyous sounds we heard the faint train whistle one more time. Jill blew a kiss to the dolphins and the sea. I grabbed her by the wrist, and together we dashed bare-footed through the sand, up the cement steps, and through the gift shop. The conductor was just lifting the footstool and giving the all-clear sign when Jill and I blasted out on the landing and cried out, "Wait!"

"Almost missed the train, ladies," the conductor said.

"No, we almost missed the moment," Jill said with her fabulous, free-spirited laugh following me into the train compartment.

We bustled our way back to our seats as the chugging motion of the train began. Our faces were bright as sunbeams. Our hair was wild and crazy from the sprint in the wind. The sedate passengers in our car gave us strange looks.

Jill didn't seem to mind them a bit as she took her seat. "That was awesome," she said, alive with glee. "How incredible! Wow!"

I nodded, still catching my breath. My heart continued to

race. We twisted in our seats as the train pulled away from the Kaikoura station, and we strained to see another glimpse of the surfers.

On the table, invisible, but definitely left there from before the train had stopped, was the possibility of my going back to school. The possibility of my becoming a speech therapist.

At that moment, anything seemed possible.

Two days later, I confided in Tony all the thoughts I'd pondered during the last part of the train ride. The morning was crisp, and I'd joined him on his walk to work so we would have a chance to talk. The last two days he had been working extra hours, and I wasn't ready to present the topic of going back to school until I had his complete attention.

"What do you think?" I asked after I'd spilled out all my ideas for school options.

"Go for it." Tony leaned over and planted a kiss on the crown of my head. My husband is gifted at seeing the big picture and editing it down to its most concise form. I knew I had his blessing, and it was up to me to think it through from there.

Later that day I sat with Dorothea for four hours and told her everything about the trip. This time, Mr. Barry didn't hide discreetly in the kitchen. He pulled up a chair and listened to my stories about Evan, the singing punter; Hika, the descendant of a Maori warrior; and Jill, the dolphin chaser.

I stopped in the middle of my description of the calm-water crossing we had on the ferry and realized that what I enjoyed about the getaway hadn't been the sights we had seen or the foods we had tried. The experience was rich because of the people.

He tangata, he tangata, he tangata.
It's the people, it's the people, it's the people.

I spent the next few days thinking a lot. When the rain kept me inside on Thursday, I sat in our one comfortable chair for many hours listening to the pings on the garage's roof. I had two medical books Mr. Barry had loaned me when I told him I was eager to learn more about what happens when a person has a stroke. When Tony came home, I summarized for him everything I'd learned. I couldn't believe how energized I felt.

The next morning, I toted my umbrella and took off on the slick sidewalk to meet Jill at the Chocolate Fish. I anticipated a long, leisurely, all-morning conversation, but Jill started off with a question that redirected everything.

"I have a huge favor to ask," she said as soon as we took our places at what had become "our" table by the window.

"Whatever it is, the answer is yes."

"You better wait until you hear what I'm asking."

Before Jill could say anything else, Tracey came over to our table with grand "hallos!" and lots of hugs. Pulling up a chair, she looked at us and said, "Do tell all. I've been dying to hear about your trip."

Jill and I took turns with the highlights, as Tracey listened intently.

"You girls have it made," she said brightly. "Where are you off to on your next lark?"

"We don't have any plans," I answered for both of us. "But wherever it might be, you'll have to come with us."

"Right!" Tracey paused before adding, "Or we could just drive around town and see how many lawn ornaments we can run over."

The three of us shared a great laugh.

Tracey stood and pushed in her chair. "The kitchen calls!"

With a more serious expression she added, "This is my place for now. My time will come to flit around like you two, but for now I belong here. For you two, this is the time of your lives to have the time of your lives."

Tracey left Jill and me at our window table with a flippant, "Ta!"

I looked back at Jill. She was biting her thumbnail.

"So, what were you going to ask me before Tracey came over?"

She took a sip of her mocha latte. "I had such a great time in Christchurch."

"I did, too."

"So much has changed for me since you showed up here, Kathy. And that's part of why I want to ask this favor of you. I was going to ask on our way home on the train, but I didn't want to sound like I was imposing."

"You? Imposing? Never." I knew what it was like to suddenly feel flustered when everything was going great. Apparently neither of us was willing to push too far in one direction or another and risk upsetting the balance that had come to us so easily at the beginning of our relationship.

"Okay, here it is. My niece is getting married next weekend. I told my brother-in-law I would come, and I know they're counting on me, but ever since I mailed back the RSVP card, I've been trying to think of how to decline."

"You don't want to go?"

Jill closed her lips, hesitating before quietly saying, "I want to go. I just don't want to go by myself."

"I'd be glad to go with you."

"Well, there's another little detail you should know before you agree. The wedding is in Sydney."

Eleven

ustralia?" I asked. "The wedding is in Sydney, Australia?"

Jill nodded. "James was planning to go with me, but now he's pulling back because of exams."

I'd met Jill's youngest son, James, the day I went to her home to book our on-line tickets for Christchurch. He was a tall, good-looking young man with dark, expressive eyes. He seemed intently interested in everything his mother had to say, which I thought was amazing and admirable.

Then I realized that James probably had been trying to fill the void his father had left and was trying to be responsive to his mom's concerns.

"I told James I'm fine going to the wedding by myself. It's a very small family affair, which is why my brother-in-law was so persuasive about James and me being there. We're the closest relatives on his side in this hemisphere, and there's no reason for me not to go."

"But…" I tried to draw out of Jill what she was thinking but not saying.

"But I don't think I want to go to Australia by myself. Traveling is the last 'alone' thing I've had to tackle. I didn't think anything of the trip when James was planning to go, but now…"

"Jill, you don't have to say anything else. I would love to go with you."

"Really?"

"Yes, really. I'm sure Tony will be all for it."

"It's such short notice."

"That's okay. I don't have anything on my calendar I need to cancel."

Jill still looked hesitant, as if she were asking too much of me.

"Hey." I reached across the table and gave her hand a squeeze. "Relax, it's dolphin time. The sun is shining; the surf is up. Let's ride the wave together. What did Tracey just tell us? This is the time of our lives to have the time of our lives. We're going to Sydney!"

A smile came to Jill's face.

I told her about one of my longtime friends in California who had been sending e-mails to me via Tony's work e-mail. "Last time she wrote, she said that I'm supposed to have an extra adventure for her. See? I have to go to Australia with you so she can vicariously experience the adventure."

"Well, then, since she's counting on it, I guess we can't let her down. You won't have to go to the wedding, if you don't want, and we can stay several extra days to play."

As I predicted, Tony was all for the excursion. He drove Jill and me to the airport the next Friday and added his encouragement for us to have the time of our lives.

I kissed him good under Gollum's gruesome gaze, grabbed

my gear, and followed Jill into the Wellington airport for the second time that month.

The clerk at the flight desk asked to see my visa. I pulled out my credit card and handed it to him.

"No, your visa, if you don't mind," he said in a weary voice, as if one too many travelers had pulled the same prank on him. I wasn't trying to pull a prank. I only had one credit card, and it was the Visa I held out to him.

Jill leaned closer. "He means your visitor's visa for Australia."

"We can buy our visitors' visas here, can't we?" she asked the clerk.

"Yes, of course. And how would you like to pay for that?"

I held out my credit card for the second time. "May I pay for my visa with my Visa?"

Jill stifled a giggle by coughing to cover it up. The clerk took my credit card without comment. Some sort of giggle enzyme must have kicked in at that point. I tried to swallow the impulse to burst out laughing and kept my mouth shut, as Jill and I purchased our visas with our Visas.

From then on, everything seemed funny to me. Maybe it was like a nervous tick. Or perhaps that's what happens when two mama chicks start flapping their wings. All the feather fluttering turns into a merciless tickling of each other's funny bones.

Once we were on the plane with seat belts fastened, Jill adjusted the magazines in the pocket in front of her to make more room to cross her legs. A bag fell out of the cloth pocket and landed on my foot. I leaned over to pick up what I assumed was the airsick bag and was surprised to see it was a mailer to send in film for developing.

The top of the bag had two statements in bold red and

orange letters. The first statement read, "Introductory Photo Offer Only $5.99." The second announcement was, "If affected by motion sickness, please use this bag."

I laughed and showed the bag to Jill. "Talk about making practical use of a bag! You can either use it to get sick, or you can use it to mail in your film."

"But it probably shouldn't be used for both," Jill said. "Oh, look at this line: 'Please take this bag with you and pass on to family or friends.'"

I looked closer and read the rest of the sentence for her. "…pass on to family or friends if you are unable to use.' That's a very important phrase: *if* you are unable to use, then you should pass it on."

"Right, because if you did use the bag, not for the film developing option but for the *other* option, you might not want to pass it on to your family or friends."

We laughed so hard neither of us could stop. It was silly. I didn't care if people were staring at us. Jill and I were off on a lark, and this was only the warm-up.

The giggle enzymes were at peak effervescence as we tried not to laugh at the flight attendant who pointed out the emergency exits with the routine dignified pose of her two fingers stuck together.

I asked Jill for a tissue to wipe my dripping nose, and she offered me the photo developing bag, which we tore in half and shared in the absence of tissue.

"I don't think any of my family or friends would like me to pass this on to them now." Jill folded up her bit of damp paper sack. "I'm not sure what to do with it."

I rifled through my magazine pocket, pulled out my photo bag and turned it into a trash receptacle.

"Yet another use for the amazing, multipurpose, mail-in-your-film-developing-slash-motion-sickness bag." Jill said.

Giggles spent, we settled in like more respectable adults, as the pilot announced that this would be a three-hour and forty-minute flight.

"You know, I always pictured Australia and New Zealand right next to each other," I said. "I didn't realize they were so far apart."

"When you meet my brother-in-law, don't tell him that's what you think of Australia. He's lived there for thirty years and considers himself an Aussie."

I noticed that Jill said the word *Aussie* the same way I would say *Ozzie,* as in *Ozzie and Harriet.*

"They really are two different countries on two different continents," Jill said. "Kiwis and Aussies don't link themselves together."

"Well, that's good to know before I try out my New Zealand slang in Sydney."

"And exactly what New Zealand slang were you thinking of trying out?" Jill had lived in Wellington for six years and still sounded like an American. I'd been there two weeks, yet I was the one collecting slang terms.

"Okay, test me on this. See if you understand my use of Kiwi terms." I cleared my throat and pieced phrases together. "Last week I went to the chemist next to the dairy and was so buggered I got the colly wobbles and had to use the dunny before I could buy my cotton buds and sticking plaster."

Jill cracked up.

"Don't laugh," I said. "Translate for me."

"Okay, let's see. Last week you went to the drugstore next to the 7-Eleven, or corner market. You were so tired that you got that nervous, queasy feeling in your stomach and had to use the restroom. Then what did you buy? Oh, wait, I remember. Q-Tips and something else."

"Plasters."

"That's right, plasters. Band-Aids. I must say, Kathy, that's pretty impressive."

"We all have our hidden talents, don't we?"

"I'm not sure that *sass* is a God-given gift, but if it is, you are doubly blessed with it."

Our flight ended with a steep landing. Since our seats were in the middle section, we couldn't see out the windows and compare the view of Sydney from the air with the view of Wellington. The little snatches of color and light I did catch from the window seemed to be lots of blue water and red-roofed houses dotted everywhere.

Jill led the way through customs where a trained dog sniffed every bag that came off the luggage carousel. We turned in our paperwork, answered questions about whether we had food, plants, or animals we were bringing into the country, and made it to the car rental booth before most of the crowd.

With a distinctly different accent from the one I'd been adjusting to in New Zealand, the rental agent asked, "Will both of you be driving, then?"

I may have jumped at the chance to drive Beatrice on an isolated, two-lane road in Wellington, but being cleared to drive on a motorway in Sydney in a rental car was too intimidating at the moment. At the risk of losing all my newly acquired "cool" status, I turned down the offer.

"No worries," the clerk said. "We'll just process this for you now."

"I'm a little nervous," Jill said to me once we were in our

small silver rental car. "I'm used to driving in Wellington, but this might be different. You keep an eye out for me, okay?"

We went slowly at first, merging into the traffic and heading for the motorway.

"Do you know where you're going?" I asked.

"Downtown. Start watching for the signs that say Sydney."

I fiddled with the map, turning it upside down and right side up until I finally found the airport and traced the route to downtown Sydney.

Looking up at the next street sign, I said, "I think we're going the wrong direction."

"Are you sure?"

"Pretty sure. See if you can exit and turn around."

I continued to track our route on the map, as Jill exited and tried to point the car in the correct direction. Due to road construction, we had to take an unexpected turn, and neither of us could figure out how to get back on the right road.

"This is a nightmare," Jill said, as we inched along through another construction zone. After fifteen minutes in the thickening traffic, she said, "It looks like we can cut over onto another highway. Can you see the name? Is it one that will take us downtown?"

"I'm not sure. Can you pull into that hotel driveway for a minute so we can look at this map together? I'm completely turned around."

The only place for our car was in front of the hotel entrance. A valet came over and opened my door.

"Oh, no. Sorry," I said. "We're not staying. Just trying to find our way."

"California girls, huh?" the young Aussie said with a tease

133

in his voice. He probably made that comment to all American women.

"Yes, as a matter of fact, we're two born-and-raised southern California girls." Jill reached for a pinch of that cheerleader charm. "And we're lost. Can you show us how to get back on the motorway? We want to go to the Vacation Inn at the Quay."

"No worries. That happens to be one of our hotels." He launched into a fast-paced set of directions complete with hand motions and a wink for each of us before he said, "G'day" and sent us on our way.

"Okay, we turn right here." Jill put on her blinker. "Then what?"

"I don't know. I couldn't understand him. I thought you understood him."

"I thought you were listening."

"I was listening." The enzyme giggles were returning. "But I didn't understand a word he said."

"Okay. You know what?" Jill checked her watch. "I'm going to return this car."

"I don't think the car is the problem."

"Very funny. I still think we should return this car."

"At the airport?"

"Yes. Look at the sign. We're right back by the airport. I'm terrible at directions, and getting lost all the time is going to ruin this trip for us. I'd rather spend the money on public transportation or a taxi and not have to worry about driving everywhere."

I appreciated Jill's candid evaluation of her weakness. Had it been me, for the sake of the money already spent, I probably would have gutted it out, gotten thoroughly frustrated, and spent the rest of the trip stressed out.

"What time is the wedding?" I checked my watch.

"At five o'clock."

"Jill, it's already four-thirty. Are you going to make it?"

"It's four-thirty in Wellington, but here it's only two-thirty because of the time change. I still have time."

I reset my watch. "Five o'clock seems like an odd time for a wedding."

"It's a short ceremony followed by a sit-down dinner. This will work out fine. We'll return the car to the rental lot, grab a cab to our hotel; I'll change and then take a cab to the wedding. It makes it easier all around."

Jill's evaluation of our car situation felt as if she were offering me freedom to change my mind about something if the situation arose. She just said things as they were and moved on. She didn't need to be right; she just needed to try possible solutions until she found the one that fit.

I liked that approach to life.

We returned our rental car to an amused rental agent and hauled our luggage around to the taxi stand.

Our driver greeted us with, "G'day!"

"Not so far," I quipped.

"No worries," he said, as Jill showed him a printout from her computer with the name and address of our hotel. Off we went, sitting in the backseat and smiling contentedly. We were prepared for a much better start to our adventure now.

Less than ten minutes later, the driver pulled up in front of a hotel and hopped out to unload our luggage for us.

"We can't be downtown at the harbor already," Jill said, looking at the reservation. Then she added a humble sounding, "Oh."

I looked at the reservation with her.

She pointed to the full name of the hotel on the computer printout. "I reserved the wrong hotel."

"It's okay," I said quickly. "It doesn't matter. We're here. We can stay at least for tonight. Otherwise you'll be late for the wedding, and that was the main reason we came."

"You're right."

Just then the hotel valet opened the back door of the cab. "Hey, the California girls are back! Coming in style this time."

Jill and I busted up.

"And this time we're staying," I said, exiting the car to show I meant it.

Jill followed me to the check-in desk and explained her reservation mistake. She asked if we could stay there one night and switch to the Vacation Inn at the Quay for the remaining three nights.

After much tapping on the computer keyboard, the young woman at the desk told us that since our reservation had been prepaid on-line through a discount site, we were unable to make any changes.

Jill's brow furrowed, but I said, "That's fine. We're here. Let's stay here."

I knew that, if I were back in the U.S., I probably would have asked to see the manager. I would have pushed for what I wanted.

But I was changing. This trip was changing me. We were, after all, in the place of "no worries," right?

When Jill whooshed out the door forty minutes later in a gorgeous blue outfit and with a whiff of gardenia-scented perfume, I walked into the bathroom and smiled at the bathtub, my favorite "no worries" machine.

Twelve

The bathtub in our Sydney hotel room was longer and higher than the standard-sized tub—and it had whirlpool jets. Having a bathtub in our hotel room was a treat for me, but having one with whirlpool jets was a double delight. I ran the water and rummaged around for something to use as bubble bath. The hotel provided shampoo, shower gel, and mouthwash in small bottles but no bubble bath.

In my cosmetic bag I carried a variety of sample-sized bath oils. Don't ask me why I brought them all the way from California. I guess I thought I'd save money when we got here by using up all the little samples.

I pulled out my collection of bottles and set them on the tub's rim. They made a nice collection. Seven different sizes, colors, shapes, and fragrances.

Checking to make sure the hotel room's door was locked, I slipped out of my clothes and put my foot in the tub to test the three inches of water. It was taking a long time to fill, but the water was just the right temperature. So I settled in and did an "eenie meenie miney mo" with the bath oils.

The purple vial won. It was lavender scented. As I poured the entire contents into the water, the purple gel sank to the bottom and sat there like a sleeping jellyfish. I broke it up with my toe, coaching it to foam up, but all it did was break into smaller jellyfish that hunkered in the tub's depths.

"Okay, so much for lavender. I'm sure the water will smell nice, but I want bubbles."

Trying bottle number two, I released a clear liquid into the water, and nothing happened. The oil floated on top of the clear water.

I went for sample number three, an amber-shaded gel that had a wonderful vanilla scent. The bubble factor was still disappointing, so I dumped in the rest of the gels. An ambrosia of bath-oil fragrances filled the air. I was pleasantly pleased with the way the green apple scent blended with the cherry almond. It would be like bathing in hot fruit punch.

As soon as the water level seemed high enough to turn on the jets, I followed the directions on the timer, set the dials, and pushed the button to make the whirlpool do its whirling wonders.

Settling into the tub, I felt the bubbles begin to rise.

Those bath gels just needed a little more agitation. I'm glad I used all of them. They were all so small. This is dreamy!

I closed my eyes and hummed to the sound of the whirlpool jets while the growing effervescence surrounded me like bubble wrap. It was a lovely, lightweight, floating sensation. I could feel airy kisses on my earlobes as runaway, tiny bubbles bid me farewell on their way to outer space. I felt as if I were being massaged by hundreds of BB-sized bubbles as they rose with the force of the jets and ever so minutely tapped my shoulders and neck.

Oh, this is nice.

The water temperature, the tub's size and shape, the wonderful fragrance that encased me, and the energetic bubbles that were filling the tub and…I felt bubbles rising to my chin and then to my mouth. Lots of bubbles.

I opened my eyes and sat up. The bubbles had gone berserk! They had formed a chain gang and were escaping the tub's high walls at an unstoppable speed. I stood in an effort to make them sink back down into the tub and not spill over onto the bathroom rug. I was fast, but they were faster. The bubbles were mutating and multiplying at a freakish rate.

Stepping out of the tub, I scooped up a handful of runaways and deposited them in the sink. Another wave came over the wall with greater speed. I scooped them up, lifted the lid to the toilet, and tried to dispose of them.

When I turned around, a league of invading bubbles had breached the tub and was coming at me across the tile floor.

Turn off the jets! Turn off the jets!

I pushed one button, then another button. Nothing happened. I tried to reset the timer. It wouldn't budge. Plunging my arm into a three-foot-deep drift of bubbles, I fished around until I found the plug and gave it a tug.

The water drained from the tub, but the bubbles had no intention of following. I noted that part of the plumbing system in this Australian bathroom was the drain in the tile floor under the sink. As the bathwater went out, I could hear it going down the drain in the tub as well as down the larger drain under the sink.

Then two things happened at once. The whirlpool jets,

which were still running because I couldn't figure out how to turn them off, were beginning to sound like they were wheezing, gasping for water. All the jets had to siphon were the bubbles.

The second thing that happened was the lavender bath gel, which had lurked on the tub's bottom, must have been among the first to go down the drain. When the purple jellyfish reached the larger drain under the sink, instead of finding their way out to sea, they decided to do what they were originally created to do. They burst into a bazillion lavender-scented bubbles and rose from the floor drain under the sink, coming at me like a fierce army of awakened sea creatures.

This is not good! Not good at all!

I stuck the plug back into the tub and turned on the water so that the whirlpool jets would have something other than bubbles to drink. As soon as the water level rose to meet the jets' begging open mouths, the newly activated layer of mighty bubbles billowed over the side of the tub like Rapunzel letting down her golden mane.

Frantically scooping up the weightless enemy by the armsful, I deposited them in the toilet until they overflowed there as well. And then I flushed. Another mistake. Any motion only made more bubbles.

Grabbing the metal wastebasket, I shoveled the bubbles that now covered the floor up to my bare ankles. When the trash can was full, I tried to empty it in the only open cavern— the bathroom sink.

That's when I caught my reflection in the bathroom mirror. I had a floof of bubbles on my head and another outcropping coming out of my shoulder that looked like an elf's cap with a bent point. The expression on my face was one of panic. I never would have recognized myself, even in a police lineup. I should have been wearing a number around my neck to match the guilt I felt for the crime of setting off a bubble bomb and endangering the life expectancy of a formerly healthy whirlpool system.

Just then the phone rang, and I nearly jumped out of my skin. That would have been a sight, because all I was wearing was my fruit punch–scented skin and an assortment of bubble patches.

Wrapping a towel around me, I quickly exited the bathroom, closing the door securely behind me.

"Hello?" My heart was pounding. I was sure the hotel manager was calling to ask why the entire sewer system was being attacked by millions of bulbous jellyfish that strangely smelled of lavender.

"Room service calling. Will you be desiring turn-down service this evening?"

"Um, no. I mean yes. Actually, I could use some more towels." I tried to calm my voice. "If that would be convenient."

"Certainly. How many would you like?"

"Oh, I don't know. How about…"

My eyes were fixed on the closed bathroom door. I couldn't finish my sentence because the worst I'd feared was happening. The bubbles were oozing out from under the door and creeping across the carpet like thousands of minuscule Navy SEALs.

"Two towels?" the woman on the other end of the phone asked.

"Actually, four would be good. No, on second thought, how about if you double that."

"Eight towels?"

"Sure, why not." It was becoming more difficult to sound

nonchalant as the bubbles inched their way toward me. "Eight towels would be fine. And you don't have to come in to turn down the beds, but if the turn-down service includes choco-lates for our pillows, I'm sure we'll make use of those."

The hotel employee obviously had been trained to remain polite in all circumstances. "And would you be wanting eight chocolates as well?"

"Sure, that would be lovely. Thank you." I hung up before she asked any more questions.

Grabbing the wastebasket under the desk, I placed it on its side in front of the bathroom door. The bubbles blithely stum-bled into the trap set for them.

Then the sweetest sound fell on my ears. It was the sound of the whirlpool jets stopping. I hoped it was because their timer had gone off and not because they had been strangled by ropes of bubbles.

Standing beside the closed bathroom door, I leaned over and listened. I'm not sure what I expected to hear. Was that the sound of thousands of bubbles bursting? Or did I only wish that bubble bursting was what was happening on the other side of the closed door? I was afraid to open the door in case the bubbles had managed to form themselves into the boogie-man. If I opened the door, he might come out, arms waving over his bubble head as he chased me around the room.

I told myself I should let the remaining bubbles calm themselves before I opened the door for inspection. I also told myself it might be good to put on more than a bath towel in case room service was speedy in delivering those towels.

As soon as I was dressed, I put the towel I'd been wearing to work, sopping up the escaped bubbles. The prisoners that had walked into my trash can trap had nearly all popped themselves. I wondered if the same phenomenon had happened behind the closed door.

It's now or never!

Turning the handle slowly, I entered the inner sanctum where everything—the tub, the floor, the toilet bowl—had a slick, glimmering sheen. If a bathroom could be glazed the way a donut is glazed, this is what it would look like.

It wasn't hard to clean up. I used every towel we had and wiped off the afterglow of the bubbles. It's possible this bathroom had never been so clean. Certainly it had never been so fragrant. I told myself I had done this hotel a favor in cleaning their bathroom so thoroughly.

Just then a knock sounded at the door. I took one last look around for unpopped bubbles before opening the door. The young woman holding the stack of towels inhaled with a look of surprise. "Mmm. It smells good in here. Like a tropical beverage."

I sniffed the air, as if I hadn't noticed. "Does it really?"

Thirteen

Jill returned to the room close to ten o'clock. I'd fallen asleep watching television but instantly revived when she stepped in. The first thing she said was, "Smells scrumptious in here. Did you have a fruit salad for dinner?"

"No, I had a fruit bath."

"What's a fruit bath?"

I told Jill the whole story, complete with all the bubbly details. She started to laugh when I described how I'd scooped the bubbles into the toilet. She kept on laughing, holding her sides, as I concluded with the comment the housekeeper made when she brought the fresh towels.

"Oh, Kathy, you're making me laugh so hard I have to go use the fruit bowl. I mean the..." she kept laughing and said, "Do you think it's safe to go in there?"

"All the bubbles are gone, if that's what you're asking. I don't think any commandos will be lurking in the corners."

Jill went in the bathroom and closed the door, but I could

Robin Jones Gunn

still hear her laughing. When she came out she said, "The funniest sight in there is all your empty bubble bath bottles lined up on the counter. Definitely evidence that a wild party went on in there. And here I was worried that you would be bored, staying in the room by yourself. Did you order anything to eat?"

"I had a chicken sandwich from room service about an hour ago. And I ate half of our chocolate mints. The other half are for you, on your pillow. So how was the wedding?"

Jill changed into yellow pajamas sprinkled with a variety of what looked like paper-doll cutouts of shoes, purses, and hats.

"The wedding was lovely. Lovely in every way. The bride was a blushing beauty, and the groom couldn't take his eyes off her. I was happy for them. Young love. There's nothing like it."

"Were you okay being there by yourself?"

"It was pretty good, actually. I thought I'd be lost at dinner, when everyone was seated as couples, but I ended up sitting beside the officiating pastor and his wife, and guess what? She was from California! Escondido. The pastor grew up here in Australia, but he and his wife live in Oregon now. Gordon and Teri were their names. They were so fun to talk with."

"I'm glad they sat with you."

"Me, too. Gordon and Teri brought me back to the hotel. I'm sure it was out of their way. I almost invited them to come up so you could meet them. I didn't because I thought you would be in bed, but here you were, having a fruit fest without me."

"Not on purpose, believe me. So how did it go with your brother-in-law?"

"Okay. Not great." Jill settled under the covers and twitched her mouth right and left before finishing her thought. "He came on pretty strong about James and me moving here."

"Here? To Sydney? You don't want to move to Sydney, do you?"

"No, I don't think so."

"Why does he think you should move here?"

"After Ray died, a lot of my family and a few close friends invited James and me to live with them. I know they meant well, but I couldn't leave Wellington right away because, well…there were some unfinished complications."

Jill paused. I waited for her to go on.

"Even after I was free to go, I didn't want to leave Wellington. I didn't want to be taken in by someone who felt sorry for us. Besides, James was already at the university. I'm sure I could leave him and he'd be fine, but I'm settled in Wellington. At least for now."

"I'm sure you've thought about going back to California."

"Lots of times. I don't know if that's what I'm supposed to do. I have this small feeling that I'm not done with Wellington yet. I think my brother-in-law feels responsible to do something for me. He and his wife are great people, but I don't want them to be my umbrella. Does that make sense?"

I nodded. "You want to be under your own parasol."

Jill nibbled on her thumbnail and then she got the correlation. "Like the parasol light at the B&B. Yes, that's a good way of saying it. For now, I feel like I need to be under my own parasol."

I tried to imagine what it must be like to be a widow at such a young age. One of my friends in California who had divorced recently told me she hadn't counted on the loneliness. I couldn't imagine my life without Tony. I knew I didn't appreciate him enough.

"Jill, may I ask you something?" I wasn't sure if the time was right, but I asked anyway. "When you want to tell me, I want to hear the whole story."

"The whole story?"

"Yes, the whole story about how Ray died."

Jill didn't look at me. She kept biting her thumbnail.

"I'm not saying you need to tell me now. Just whenever you want to. And if you don't want to, that's fine, too."

"Hasn't Tony said anything about it?"

"No."

She looked surprised.

"And I won't ask him, either." I looked directly at her. "Even if he does know, I'd rather hear everything from you. If and when you want to talk about it."

"I don't think I'm ready to do that tonight," she said in a small voice.

"That's okay. This is an open invitation. Definitely a come-as-you-are sort of invitation. No obligations attached."

I expected Jill to cry as we talked about Ray, but she didn't. Her smooth, fair skin took on a glow, and her expression was one of gratitude. "Thank you, Kathy. I will tell you sometime. Just not tonight."

"No worries," I said, trying to sound lighthearted.

We settled in for a cozy night's sleep. I felt as if an invisible sweetness had strung itself like a clothesline between Jill and me in our twin beds. When laundry day came, I had no doubt Jill would hang up the personal unmentionables of her life story. And I would be there to hold the line for her.

In the morning we opted for breakfast in the hotel restaurant instead of room service. We thought that route would prompt us to get up and dressed and out the door instead of lounging in our pj's and eating breakfast in bed.

The restaurant offered a buffet breakfast, and we filled our plates with many of the foods we would find at home in California. I had scrambled eggs, toast, and bacon that was flat and thick and not very crinkled or crispy. Stopping at the juice and condiment table, we reached for plastic, individual-sized tubs of butter and jelly.

"What's this?" I asked Jill, holding up a tiny tub of something called Vegemite.

"You should try it."

"But what is it?"

"I can't tell you."

"What do you mean you can't tell me? Don't you know what it is?"

"Oh, I know all right. In New Zealand our brand is Marmite."

"Your brand of what?"

"Just try it."

I followed Jill back to our table and kept pestering her. "Is it like peanut butter?"

"No."

"Honey?"

"What, dear?" Her expression let me know that my goofy wit was beginning to rub off on her.

"Just answer me this, Miss Smarty Party. What are you supposed to do with Vegemite?"

"Well, different people have different opinions of what should be done with Vegemite." Her poker face was starting to crack at the corners of her mouth. "I will simply tell you that you should try it and see what you think. I will also tell you that it's considered a comfort food."

"Like chocolate?"

"I can't really answer that."

"So do I spoon it on my eggs or what?"

"Try it on your toast," Jill suggested.

Eager to get this silly game over with, I peeled back the top and spread all of the dark molasses-colored Vegemite on half a slice of toast. It had the consistency of jellified honey and smelled like Worcestershire sauce.

"Are you sure people eat this? I mean, it's safe for ingestion, right?"

"Yes. Just try a bite."

I did. Never in my life had I experienced such a disagreeable explosion of confused tastes on my poor tongue. It was a challenge to make myself swallow the whole bite.

"I don't care for it." I politely put the slice of toast to the side of my plate and made a face.

Jill was laughing now. This had been good fun for her.

"I'm sure you were making up the part about its being comfort food. What is it, really? Condensed sushi? Purse-sized shoe polish?"

"No, it's really, truly a type of spread for bread or whatever, and it's really, truly considered comfort food."

I shook my head, refusing to believe her. "Then my taste buds have not yet flipped down under because I…" instead of finishing my sentence, I demonstrated my shoulder-shaking dislike of the goo and downed my orange juice in one gulp.

Jill bowed her head to pray over our breakfast. "Lord, for what Kathy is about to swallow, may she be truly grateful. Amen."

"That was rude!" I teased her.

"I know. I was just giving you a hard time. I'll really pray now."

I bowed with her while my tongue made a clean sweep of the inside of my mouth. This time when Jill said, "Amen," I had no problem agreeing with her and adding my amen as well.

Enjoying the rest of my breakfast, I picked up the Vegemite wrapper and said, "You know what this reminds me of?"

"I don't think I want to know."

"No, I mean the name. Remember the *I Love Lucy* episode where she's trying to do a commercial for some elixir she keeps drinking until it makes her tipsy?"

"Oh, yeah. Vetavitavegamita."

"No," I said. "It was Meatavitavegamin."

"No, Vitametavegamite."

"No, I think it was Vegamitavitamita."

"That's not it. All I remember was Lucy's line, 'It's so tasty, too!'" Jill laughed. "I'm guessing you wouldn't apply that same line to this sample of Vegemite."

"Vitameatavegamin!" I said with the snap of my fingers. "That's it!"

"If you say so. Come on, Lucy. We have some sights to see."

The concierge provided us with a map along with several brochures containing details on what to do in Sydney. He greeted us with, "G'day," and said, "No worries" twice before showing us how to get to the train station, which was the closest form of public transportation and only two blocks away.

Bright autumn sun laced with a soft breeze greeted us as Jill and I walked in step. The temperature felt warmer than when we had left Wellington. A tall palm tree shaded the small train station where we bought two tickets to the Quay, which the map indicated was the main harbor area. I was eager to see the famous Sydney Opera House. Jill had some definite opinions about the art museum.

"I'm glad we're not driving," she said, as the two of us boarded the quaint train. The seating area we settled in felt similar to a subway. Across from us a little boy with a gleeful Australian accent was trying to snatch a piece of candy out of his grandpa's hand. Three teenage girls in belly button–revealing T-shirts were discussing what they should buy for another girl's birthday gift. I agreed with Jill about not having a car. I liked getting a touch of Aussie Saturday life on the public transportation.

The train rolled into the station near the Quay. Jill and I followed the crowd off the train, past some tourist shops, and into an open area bustling with movement. Visitors and locals strolled in the sunshine and dined at the open-air cafés. Others rushed to get on one of the many ferries and other touring boats that docked in the long harbor at what was labeled the Circular Quay.

We turned to the right, and there stood the Opera House, white and elegant against the seamless blue sky at the end of Sydney Harbor. The sight took my breath away.

"I've seen pictures of this landmark for years." I flipped up my sunglasses to get a better look as we walked toward it. "But this is really something. It reminds me of a huge ship with its sails at full mast."

"And the bridge." Jill pointed to the left. "Do you recognize that? Think of how many times we've seen fireworks being launched from that bridge. And there it is!"

I was glad that Jill didn't feel embarrassed to play tourist with me. I wanted to see everything.

"Let's see if we can buy tickets for whatever performance is playing at the Opera House," Jill suggested.

We headed for the great alabaster structure, and I commented that the area we were walking through had a southern California feel to it. I smiled when I heard the familiar ring of a cell phone nearby. It even sounded like the personalized tune on my phone.

That's when I realized it was my phone. Skyler was calling from college to tell me she had landed the summer job she had hoped for on campus in the admissions office.

"I'm thrilled for you, Sky! That's great news!"

"Thanks, Mom. So, what are you doing? Washing Dad's jeans and hanging them outside in the rain again?"

"No, as a matter of fact, I'm walking up the steps toward the entrance of the Sydney Opera House."

Skyler didn't respond.

"Are you still there?"

"You can't be serious," she said. "You're in Sydney? Australia? *The* Australia that I've wanted to go to since I was, like, seven?"

"Yes, that very same Australia. I came over here yesterday with Jill. She had to go to a wedding, and we thought we'd have a little getaway. Dad said he was going to send you an e-mail. Didn't you get it?"

"No, my computer isn't working. But don't worry. I have a guy who's working on it for me and…" with a giggle she added, "he's really cute!"

It felt good to hear my daughter's voice and her giggle. Before we hung up she begged me to buy certain Australian souvenirs for her—and, oh yes, she promised to pay me back. She ended with, "Mom, did you know that you are the coolest?"

"Coolest what?"

"You are the coolest world-traveling, God-loving, adventure-taking mother on this planet. When I grow up I want to be exactly like you!"

I closed my cell phone with my head in the clouds. Skyler's words across the miles and across the continents made up for all the times in high school that she had rolled her eyes and given me that get-a-life look.

The truth was, I *had* gotten a life, and suddenly I was cool. My life was flipped. Flipped completely down under. And I wasn't sure I ever wanted it to flop back to the way it had been.

Fourteen

What surprised me the most about the Sydney Opera House was the immensity of the building. I felt as if a great fish were swallowing us when we went inside. Jill read to me from the tour brochure that the building was finished in 1973 and had gone ninety-five million dollars over budget. Neither of us, even with our familiarity with the film industry, could imagine a project going so far over budget.

The part that surprised us the most was that the building wasn't a single, huge concert hall but rather a complex with several performing arenas. We found that we could buy tickets on the spot and go to an opera that evening, a jazz concert later in the afternoon, or a Shakespearean performance at seven. The system was much less formal than anything I'd experienced in the U.S.

We both agreed on tickets for the opera, even though we knew nothing about the performance being presented that evening. It just seemed that, when at the Opera House, go to the opera.

"What would you think about going to the art museum now?" Jill asked, unfolding the map the concierge had given us. "I read in the tour brochure that it has some extraordinary Aboriginal art. It's not far from here. We could walk through the botanical gardens."

"Sure!" I was still euphoric about being "cool," according to Skyler. Jill could have asked if I wanted to walk across the top of the harbor bridge attached to nothing but a bungee cord, and I would have done it.

The botanical gardens were brimming with autumn flowers still in bloom and a wealth of imposing old trees. The sun was warm enough to prompt us to peel off our sweaters. Jill pulled up her hair in a ponytail, and we talked about how much we loved the weather.

At a split in the trail, we stopped where half a dozen people were standing and staring up into a huge tree. The tree was thick with what looked like black pods the size of kittens hanging from the branches.

"What are you looking at?" Jill came alongside an older man who had a pair of binoculars.

"Bats." He handed her the binoculars. "Fruit bats. Curious creatures."

I immediately took several steps backward as a shiver ran up my spine. Jill peered through the binoculars and made appreciative comments about how clearly she could make out the details of the bats' folded-up wings.

From where I stood, I could easily see that this horde of nocturnal creatures was hanging upside down. There had to be hundreds of them. A young man with a backpack picked up a stone and threw it up into the tree. A great fluttering sound followed.

Jill and I instinctively grabbed each other by the arm and took off running away from the disturbed bats. Behind us we heard the older man yelling at the rock thrower.

"Are they following us?" I squealed. I couldn't bring myself to turn around and look.

"No, they're going back to the tree."

We slowed our pace to a walk and joined in a burst of nervous laughter.

"That was too creepy," I said with a shiver. "I'm going to have nightmares about bats chasing me."

Jill playfully reached over and fluttered the back of my hair with her hand, as if imitating the sensation of a bat hiding in my tresses.

"Not funny! Not funny! Not funny!" I spouted, pulling away.

"You're not fond of bats, I take it."

"You're quick!" I teased her back.

Jill chuckled and pointed to where we exited the botanical gardens to connect with the art museum. "How did you handle Batman while you were growing up?"

"Never watched it. Never went to see the Batman movies. Wouldn't let my daughter keep any Batman-related miniature action figures that came with her kid's meal. Bats are awful. Bats are evil. Bats should never be made into toys for children to play with or appreciated in any way, shape, or form!"

Jill laughed.

"Why are you laughing? Bats are not funny. They are wicked."

"Okay! Well, it's unfortunate you don't feel the freedom to express your *true* opinion on the topic."

We walked another few yards before I turned the tables. "So, what are you afraid of?"

"Nothing," Jill said with an all-too-cocky kick in her step, as we entered the stately art museum. While we rode the escalator to the lower level to view the Yiribana Gallery, I told Jill she couldn't get off that easily. There had to be something she was afraid of.

"Hobbits." She winked.

"That joke doesn't work here. We're done with the hobbit jokes. I'll find out what you're frightened of one of these days, and then I'll demonstrate how an understanding friend should treat another friend's phobias."

Jill took off a few steps ahead of me with a carefree flip of her hand, as if she didn't have a fright in the world. I knew it was only a matter of time.

Taking one look at the art in front of us, I thought we were in the wrong wing. Jill, however, offered low, appreciative humming sounds and drew closer to the pictures.

"These are exceptional," she murmured, gazing at one of the many walls lined with large canvases. Each of the paintings was made up of thousands and thousands of perfectly round dots all placed so as to form a pattern. The colors were earth colors: sand, green, blue, black.

"Don't you love this? It's like a bird's eye view on an ancient world but with so much energy that it seems to move."

I had to do a double take to make sure Jill wasn't joking. Trying to sound as polite as possible, I said, "I don't think I'm seeing what you're seeing."

Jill did a double take on me to make sure I wasn't joking. "It's all about the balance. That's the beauty of how the Aborigines view the world. Look at this one."

Jill explained the way the dots lined up to form shapes and impressions of shape. She gave me a crash course on how

Aboriginal art compared with the European Impressionists, including a side note on how Monet captured light and time of day with his many water lily paintings. Jill saw much more in these paintings than I did and kept talking about the balance.

When she finally used the word *geometry*, I confessed that I didn't like math. I'd never liked math.

Jill lifted an eyebrow in disbelief. "Without math, how would we have art?"

She lost me on that one. I saw art as a free expression of color and shape, and as something I definitely wasn't gifted in. Words came easier to me. Tony used to say that one-liners were my art form.

It wasn't as if having sassy one-liners on the tip of my tongue was necessarily a gift, but for some reason as we strolled past another row of Aboriginal art, I felt compelled to think about how to make use of my own strange art.

"What does this art say to you?" Jill asked.

"I don't know if it says anything specific. It reminds me of pottery."

"Pottery," Jill repeated. Obviously the comparison had never entered her mind. "What kind of pottery?"

"Navajo."

We rounded a corner and came into a room with an umbrella-style clothesline set up against the back wall. Jill burst out laughing, but I didn't.

From the clothesline hung a hundred papier-mâché bats, all linked to the clothesline wire with their toes, and all of them cocooned by their wings. The wings were delicately painted the same way the pictures had been with various rows of color-ful dots. Each bat was different.

Or so Jill said.

I stayed far away from the clothesline bats, even though I knew they were too colorful to be real. They still spooked me. I already was fighting with my sense of being watched every time I hung our clothes outside on the line. I didn't want to entertain even the slightest thought that a bat, decorative or real, might appear one day, hanging from the clothesline when I walked outside with a basket of laundry.

"Come on." Jill cheerfully tugged on my sleeve. "You might enjoy some of the paintings upstairs a little more."

We wandered through the high-ceilinged rooms, admiring what I referred to as masterpieces. Many of the huge, detailed paintings that lined the walls were originals by artists whose names I recognized like Dante Gabriel Rossetti. The Victorian women these artists painted were round and fair skinned with diaphanous gowns and flowers in their flowing blond hair. They represented the idealized, romanticized woman and were everything I had grown up wishing I could be.

We strolled through more rooms where I saw a picture of a landscape with creamy-colored sheep. Jill saw a harmony of sky and earth in a sixty-forty ratio. I saw a picture of a woman darning socks. Jill saw a median line that intersected at the woman's eyes and not her hands.

Somewhere between a dark and mystical oil of St. Francis of Assisi and a colorful rendition of the Parable of the Ten Virgins, I started to glimpse what Jill saw. What made the art beautiful wasn't so much the subject of the painting but rather the balance of lines and color used to present the subject.

"It's not so much what happens inside the frame," Jill said in a final explanation of how math defines art. "But how balanced the subject is. That's what makes the scene beautiful to our way of viewing it."

I was enjoying the tour with my own personal art appreciation instructor, but I was slow to let Jill know how cool I thought she and her insights were. After all, she kept using math terms to make her point.

One scene of a Victorian woman bending to pick up a seashell caught our attention and caused both of us to stop and appreciate it for our own separate reasons. The image inside the round center of the gold frame was dressed in a creamy, loose-fitting dress that was accented with blue embroidery around the hem and flouncy sleeves. Her feet were covered with delicate sandals. In the distance all that could be seen was a faint peninsula that shaped the boundary of the calm bay.

"What do you see?" Jill asked.

"An elegant woman standing on a deserted beach. I love her dress and the serenity of her posture. She gives the appearance of having all the time in the world to stroll along the beach and examine shells."

"It's definitely a beach from this side of the world," Jill said. "You can tell by the color of the sand, the water, and the cliffs in the background. Those are down under shades. That woman belongs there. That's her beach. She's not just visiting. She walks that sand daily looking for treasures."

Apparently Jill was getting a personal message from the painting. I sat down on the wide bench in the middle of the gallery for those wanting to contemplate a painting. I chose, instead, to contemplate Jill.

"What do you see in this picture?" I asked.

Jill tilted her head.

"All the lines in the picture direct us to whatever she's holding in her hand. And that treasure is kept hidden from our view because she hasn't opened her hand all the way."

Turning to face me, Jill said in clear, precise words, "I hold a treasure in my hand. But I don't know what it is."

"A talent, maybe? A gift? A passion for something?" I wasn't sure I knew her well enough to guess what that hidden passion might be. However, I knew whatever it was, she was closer to discovering it now than she had been for many months. Perhaps many years. She had changed so much in the few weeks I'd known her.

We continued to gaze at the picture. I was beginning to see the lines, the symmetry, and the median angles. Those lines didn't ruin my appreciation for the subject but rather made me aware of how right Jill was about the necessity of geometry.

Jill had said something earlier about how art is most beautiful when it's balanced. Dark and light. Intense and subtle. I wondered if she saw the same balance in life. The heaviness she had carried the past two years was now giving way to a lightness in her spirit.

"Do you mind if we stop by the gift shop?" Jill asked, when we started to leave the museum a short time later.

I never objected to shopping. I bought a poster-sized copy of the Victorian woman on the beach while Jill bought a postcard of the same print along with a dozen postcards of the Aboriginal art.

"Do you think you might frame that?" Jill asked.

"Yes, I was thinking of hanging it over our bed. You've seen the picture Mr. Barry has there now. It's a big bunch of tropical flowers. Ever since I took the obnoxious bedspread off the bed, the picture feels out of place."

What I didn't tell Jill and knew I would never tell Tony was that in a peculiar way I missed the old bedspread. The one I had bought on a shopping trip with Jill was similar to the one I had at home. The muted tones of the new, pale yellow bed-spread would go nicely with the colors in the picture. But once I'd gotten the quieter colors on our bed, the garage seemed smaller. Duller. The bright bedspread had been the inescapable focal point of the room, but at least it gave the room a focal point. I knew that after Jill's art lesson, I'd be sizing up our apartment with a new eye for balance and looking for "inter-sections of repeated colors." I doubted that any of my decorating attempts from here on out would be easy unless I gave consideration to the importance of geometry.

"Remind me to give you a lesson in something later," I said, as we left the gift shop.

"Okay. A lesson in what?"

"I don't know yet. Something that will make you feel more informed yet leave you with the feeling that your life was less complex before you learned that lesson."

"Okay," Jill said hesitantly. "And before you decide what torturous lesson you're going to teach me, are you in the mood for more shopping?"

"Sure. Shopping I can do painlessly."

"Or are you hungry? Because if you want to eat, according to this map, I think we could walk to a place called Woolloomooloo and go to a place that serves *pie floaters*."

"And exactly what is a pie floater?"

"It says here it's a meat pie swimming in a bowl of pea soup."

Jill and I exchanged grimaces.

She looked back at the tour book and added, "Served with a kangaroo tail as a spoon."

Fifteen

I was only kidding about the kangaroo tail spoons." Jill laughed at the shocked expression on my face. "But the rest of the description is what it says right here."

I grabbed the book out of her hand. "Do they have any recommendations for one of those cafés by the water we passed earlier? Not that I'm against meat pies swimming in pea soup or anything, but the Vegemite was enough of a stretch for my taste buds this morning."

"Let's walk back to the harbor and see what strikes our fancy." Jill snatched the map back from me. "I think it's shorter if we go this way."

As we walked, I playfully asked, "Should I be questioning your sense of direction after the way we drove around in the rental car?"

"No. I'm much better on foot than I am behind the wheel. And before you say anything, Miss Kathy Girl, I happen to know how safe you are behind the wheel as well!"

We only made it two blocks before seeing a store with outback gear in the window.

"Wait, Jill. Skyler wanted a hat. An outback hat. Do you mind if we stop in here?"

Jill didn't seem to mind stopping to shop anytime, anywhere.

When we first entered the store, I was distracted from looking for a hat because the first thing I saw was a case of Australian opals in a variety of jewelry settings. A pair of light blue opal earrings in a silver setting looked like something Skyler might like, even if it wasn't something she had asked me to buy for her. I tried to figure out the price in U.S. dollars while Jill shopped for hats.

"What do you think of this one?" Jill tried on a khaki green hat that flipped up on the side and had a tie that hung far below her chin.

"It's a little manly, don't you think? Maybe something smaller."

"Actually, this one is the Manly hat." The clerk stepped closer and handed Jill a wide-brimmed hat made from neutral canvas.

"It looks like a beach hat," I said, wondering what the joke was since my husband wouldn't consider anything "manly" about such a hat.

"Exactly," the clerk agreed. "A Manly Beach hat."

We looked around at a few other items and then exited without buying anything, feeling a bit worn down from the confusing exchange.

"Have no fear," Jill said. "I can see another shop less than a block from here. We'll find a hat for Skyler before the sun goes down."

We made our way back to the harbor—one gift shop at a time. I was relieved that Jill enjoyed shopping as much as I did.

For me, half the fun was trying on every hat and comparing prices on all the opals. I always felt better about a purchase when I knew I'd gotten a good deal.

"Look at these little kangaroos!" Jill said, as we entered one of the gift shops near the Quay. "They even squeak! I'm buying this one with the Australian flag."

She picked up a stuffed mama kangaroo with a joey peeping out of her pouch. "Oh, and this one has to come home with me. My granddaughter needs it."

Between the two of us, we snatched up all nine of the little kangaroos and started trying on more hats. I'd plopped at least a dozen on my head, but all the outback ones were pretty large and heavy.

"What do you think of this hat?" Jill put on one that looked more feminine than the others.

"That's cute. If Skyler doesn't like it, I'd wear it." I took the hat from Jill and tried it on.

"Sold," I said without even looking at myself in a mirror. This was the first hat of the day that wasn't too big for a woman-sized head.

I took the hat and stuffed kangaroos to the counter and noticed another shopper browsing by the jewelry case. She was comparing her opal necklace with a silver one on display.

"That's very pretty." I nodded at her necklace.

"Oh, thanks." Her accent sounded southern. "I just bought it at the Rock. They only had gold over there. I like this silver one better. Have you been to the Rock yet?"

"No, where is that?"

"Other side of the harbor. Darling shops. And they have a flea market going on. My husband bought himself a pair of leather boots. You should go over there."

"You called it the Rock?"

"That's right. Isn't that right, honey?"

Her husband stepped in and said, "It's the Rocks, not the Rock. It's the oldest part of Sydney, right off the harbor, where the convicts landed in colonial times. The store we liked was on Lower Fort Street."

"Thanks. We'll go there next."

Leaving the store with Skyler's girlish outback hat and a bagful of kangaroos, we hailed a cab and asked to be taken to the Rocks. We were still in a shopping mood, and time was of the essence. When we reached Lower Fort Street, we did a little opal jewelry browsing before making our way down the uneven brick streets to the Saturday market.

The brick buildings around us seemed to hold in their secrets of rowdier times in this square. Today, artisans—not Great Britain's undesirables—filled the Rocks.

I bought a Christmas ornament at the first stall we passed and paused to try some organic hand lotion. The woman who created the lotion showed me her line of soaps, shampoos, and bath oils.

"Step away from the bubble bath." Jill teased, as she came up from behind and pretended to be on patrol. "You know what happened the last time you had several bottles within reach. Just put down the bath oil, and nobody gets hurt."

I chortled and said I was sampling the lotion. I held out my hand for Jill to sniff the sweet fragrance.

"Nice. Plumeria," Jill said.

"We call it frangipani," said the clerk.

"We'd like two bottles," I told the woman.

"I should get one, too," Jill said.

"No, that's why I'm buying two. One is for you."

Jill put her wallet back in her purse and gave me a tender look. "Thank you, Kathy."

"You're welcome."

Jill looked as if it had been a long time since anyone had surprised her with a little gift.

We headed toward another stall where a man was playing what the sign called a didjeridoo. He blew into the end of a long, hollow tube, and the vibrating sound that came from the primitive instrument filled the area with a rounded sort of hum.

As we watched him play, we noticed three women who had to be at least our age, dressed like underwater ballet swimmers but with some comic twists. They wore brightly-colored swim caps that had plastic flowers attached to their sides, orange swimmer's goggles, one-piece bathing suits in matching blue with yellow and pink polka dots, matching blue tights on their legs, and pink jelly sandals. Their waists were decked out with inflatable kiddy inner tubes that had yellow duckies on the blue circles. The women's arms were adorned with blown-up, bright yellow floaties.

One woman had a snorkel in her mouth and was making exaggerated gurgling noises. The other two women were calling out the strokes, "And one, two, turn to the side, three, arms up, and four."

Jill and I, along with a dozen others, stopped to stare at the bizarre street theater company. The three women, in perfectly synchronized motions, treated the open air as their practice swimming pool and moved through the crowd performing their routine as smoothly as any dance ensemble. Trailing behind them was another woman in a gray shark costume, blowing bubbles through the shark's wide-open mouth. They were having a ball.

Jill and I laughed even though none of the other spectators seemed to know how to react.

"Chilly, this water today, don't you think, girls?" one of the swimmers said.

"Brisk!" said the other.

"Gurffple!" said the one with the snorkel.

"Lovely day, no less. Again, ladies, from the top. Push to the surface and down…"

Off they went. Arms up, then bending at the waist, all in unison.

The gathering of curious viewers was now laughing with Jill and me. "Well, that's one way to get your exercise!" a woman said.

"Where do we sign up?" Jill asked me, as we watched the blue-legged ballerinas waddle and wiggle away from us. "That was daring and darling. I loved it!"

"Should we see about starting up our own routine and try it out in front of the Chocolate Fish?" I asked.

"I'm sure Tracey would be all for it."

"Come on, Jill! You could put those old cheerleading skills back into use."

"Thanks for the encouragement, but I don't think out-of-water ballet is the hidden treasure I hold in my hand."

We chuckled and continued our trek through the open market. We could still feel the low vibrations of the didjeridoo instrument, as it released more vibrating sounds into the air and into the earth beneath our feet.

This is a strange and wonderful place.

That same thought repeated itself throughout the afternoon. We bought a variety of fun souvenirs at the outdoor market, including a boomerang and a wooden bowl made from the burl of an aged eucalyptus tree. Jill wanted the bowl for her coffee table and was enthralled with the various lines and squiggles that showed through the sides of the polished wood. Her appreciation for the symmetry of the lines didn't bother me so much anymore. I wondered if I was beginning to make peace with math.

We found great prices on opal jewelry, and I splurged on a blue opal necklace with matching earrings for myself. The shade of blue in the stones reminded me of the blue sky over Christchurch and the inviting blue of the water in front of the Chocolate Fish. I knew that whenever I looked at the necklace, it would make me feel happy.

By four-thirty we were more than ready for something to eat and were thrilled to find an outdoor café right on the harbor that had a table open for us next to the water. Our prime seats gave us a perfect view of the bridge, the Opera House, and the ferries that came and went at a quick pace from the Quay.

"This couldn't be better!" Jill motioned to the panorama before us. "What a beautiful afternoon; the air is so warm and nice. We'll have to take a ferry ride tomorrow."

I took a drink of my iced tea. "I just thought of something. We aren't exactly dressed for the opera, and I don't think we'll have enough time to go back to the hotel to change."

"Well," Jill said, reaching into one of our shopping bags. "I think you should jazz up your outfit with this hat." She popped the outback hat on my head. "What do you think?"

"Hey, be nice. I like this hat!"

"I do, too. It looks great on you. I think Skyler may have to come here herself and pick out her own hat."

Reaching into one of my shopping bags, I pulled out several of the stuffed kangaroos. "We could skin these little critters and quickly make evening gowns for ourselves out of their fur. We certainly have enough pelts to make two floor-length gowns."

Jill laughed.

At that moment I noticed a tattered white feather that had floated from one of the many birds dipping in and out of the café area. They were hopping around looking for a leftover crust or a bit of forgotten French fry. The feather landed on our table. I snatched it up and slipped it into the inside pocket of my purse.

"Grabbing a feather for the final touch on our evening wear?" Jill asked.

"I'm starting a collection," I said, reminding Jill about the two feathers that were in my hair the day we met at the Chocolate Fish. I didn't tell her that my plan was to create a greeting card with the feathers.

We clinked the rims of our iced tea glasses as the waitress stepped up to take the rest of our order. We talked her into snapping our picture, and I knew this would be the picture I would frame. I would long remember the sensations of this place and the lightness of this day.

"I heard you talking about the dress code for the opera," the waitress said when she delivered our Thai salads. "Some people dress up, but there's no dress code, so you'll be fine in what you're wearing."

"Too bad," Jill said, surprising the waitress and me. "I was hoping for an excuse to shop for something really extravagant."

"We can still do that, if we eat quickly."

"Who can eat quickly in a setting like this? I'm going to savor each bite."

I felt the same way. We watched sailboats in the harbor,

took small bites of our delicious salads, and savored each moment of the balmy Sydney evening.

Since we were so close to the Opera House, we took our time strolling over there. As we walked up the steep stairs, we saw people dressed in formal attire as well as others who were in shorts and T-shirts. This definitely was a gathering place for everyone.

Our seats were terrific. The entire theater filled with eagerly chatting guests. All around us in our section were school children that Jill and I guessed to be about eighth- or ninth-graders. All of them wore school uniforms. The boys were from one school, and the girls were from another. Both of us loved listening to the conversations and innocent flirting that was going on between the two groups. Jill and I kept exchanging grins and eyebrow-raised expressions.

The musicians took their places. The lights dimmed. The students' politeness was impressive as the room quieted, and the curtain went up.

The program called this performance "Opera Favorites," and the first song was "Nessun Dorma" from an opera called *Turandot*. A stout man delivered the song, and I knew I'd heard it before. I didn't know where, but part of the melody was familiar. On the forceful notes, the singer's voice reverberated in the rounded auditorium. When his tones grew softer, the room seemed to shrink with his voice.

I was amazed that one man's voice could fill the space so powerfully. I was also astounded that such a large group of students would be held in respectful silence as he sang. I knew very little about opera, so I'm sure I didn't appreciate the performance as much as I might have. But I doubted that a roomful of California students the same age would have given the performance the same kind of attention and appreciation.

The applause rose heartily from the crowd, as the performer took his bow. Next came an aria from *Madame Butterfly*, and again, when the woman sang, I knew I'd heard the song before. Maybe I knew a little more about opera than I'd realized.

Intermission came sooner than I expected. Most of the audience cleared out of the auditorium. Jill and I followed and found ourselves on the open deck of the lower level of the Opera House facing the harbor. When we had entered the Opera House, the evening sky was dressed in twilight. We had missed the sunset, but now, in front of this magical opening to another world, we looked out on Sydney Harbor with all the twinkle lights winking back at us.

"Everyone is so chatty!" Jill looked around.

Some of the audience were waiting in line to buy beverages. Others were leaning against the railing, pointing up at the stars that were doing their twinkling best to match the lights reflected in the harbor waters.

A lit-up ship puttered past us, with music loud enough for us to hear. We could see couples dancing on the top level. It was a splendidly romantic sight, one that would have made a fabulous subject for a beautiful photograph or, better yet, an oil painting.

Jill's profile dipped slightly. Her shoulders dropped. I saw a tear dance alone down her cheek.

"Are you okay?"

"I miss Ray," she whispered.

The only thing I knew to do was to stand with her. So I did. Shoulder to shoulder, leaning with our arms on the railing, watching the romantic scene float past us.

Sixteen

The second half of the "Opera Favorites" performance put both Jill and me in a weepy mood, and we used up all the tissues that we had between us. I didn't sense any self-pity from Jill. This was a peaceful sadness.

With few words, we took a cab back to our hotel. If there is such thing as a beautiful sorrow, that was the sensation Jill and I shared under the stars that night.

We carried our shopping bags to the elevator and arrived back at our hotel room a full fifteen hours after we had left. Unlocking the door, we both sniffed when we entered. Not from tears but because the room still smelled like a big fruit ambrosia.

The message light was blinking on our phone. Jill listened and said, "One message. From my brother-in-law. He invited us to his house for lunch tomorrow. What do you think?"

"It's up to you."

"Let's decide in the morning," Jill suggested. "It's too late to call him now anyway."

Jill decided the next morning not to see her brother-in-law. I would have been fine either way, but she told him we were going to visit a nearby church and then do some more sightseeing.

The closest church was a small community church where we were welcomed as special visitors from America and invited to stand and say a few words. Jill said a few, and I said even fewer. It turned out that even the pastor that day was visiting. His message was from a familiar passage in the Gospel of John.

After attending the same church for so many years, I enjoyed the freshness of being with this group of eighty or so faithful believers. It was a personal time of worship with nothing about the service that resembled a corporate production. This church in Sydney was similar in many ways to Jill's church in Wellington that Tony and I had visited the week before.

As Jill and I boarded the bus that stopped a few blocks from the church, I mentioned how much I enjoyed being at a small church.

"It's interesting that you would say that because I was just thinking how much I miss the megachurch we used to belong to in California. Grass is always greener on the other side of the world, isn't it?"

We headed for the harbor without a set plan of what we were going to do with the rest of the gloriously sunny day that stretched out before us. I looked through a couple of pamphlets on Sydney that I'd picked up in a rack at the hotel.

"What about going to the beach?" I asked. "We can take a ferry to a couple of different beaches, or we can take a bus to Bondi Beach."

"Sure." Jill looked over my shoulder at the map. "I don't believe it."

"What?"

"Do you remember that clerk in the first shop we went to yesterday and how he was trying to convince us that the hat he was showing us was a Manly Beach hat?"

"Yes."

"Well, look on the map. Manly Beach." Jill chuckled. "He wasn't teasing us or making it up. There really is a Manly Beach, and that was a Manly Beach hat!"

"Then that's the beach we're going to."

We got off the bus at the Quay and found the right dock for the ferry to Manly Beach. I stopped in front of the sign that read, "Manly Ferries," and wondered if anyone else thought that sounded funny.

"Come on." Jill ignored the sign. "This is the one we want. They're boarding now."

We packed into what felt like a floating, wide-bodied bus with more than a hundred other eager weekend beachgoers. The seats outside on the deck in the delicious fresh air were all taken, so Jill and I went inside and sat at the end of a long row. It felt like sitting in a movie theater except the show was all around us outside the windows.

With smooth maneuvering, the ferry pulled out of the busy dock and headed for the open bay. On both sides we could see dozens of sailboats of all sizes with passengers seizing the gorgeous day. The tall buildings that lined the harbor area began to diminish as we motored past some of the many bays and inlets of the wide, deep blue harbor.

Flipping through the tour pamphlet, I found a map and saw that we would soon be on a beach that faced east, and the water would be the Pacific Ocean. The South Pacific, to be exact. I was amazed that, after so many years of facing west to put my feet into the Pacific Ocean, I was now on the other side of that vast expanse of water. It was one of those moments in which my mind tapped into the amazement of where I was.

When we docked in Manly Cove, all the other travelers seemed to know where to go to cross the peninsula to Manly Beach. A loud, chirping sound accompanied the green crosswalk sign. We moved like an army of ants through a long outdoor mall of shops and came out at a wide, sandy beach teeming with Sunday swimmers of all ages.

Jill tapped my arm and pointed to a young man who stood a few feet away with his arms crossed and his back to us, gazing out at the water. He had on a broad-rimmed khaki beach hat like we had seen in the store yesterday. He wore red swim trunks and a tank top. On the back of the tank top, in bold letters, were the words, "Manly Lifeguard."

Jill whispered, "I wonder if that helps bolster his self-image."

Now she was ready to start with the Manly jokes. "Do you think it's a joke T-shirt, or is it real?"

"Oh, it's real," Jill said. "There's another one." She pointed to another "Manly Lifeguard" positioned in a lookout stance in the sand.

"It's good to be under the watchful eye of so many Manly Lifeguards," I said.

"I know. Especially with their Manly shoulders bulging out of their Manly tank tops."

We shared a giggle and found an open space where we could sit in the sand. Both of us had worn summer skirts and cotton blouses to church that morning. Since we didn't know we were coming to the beach on this trip, we hadn't packed our swimsuits. Not that I would have gone swimming, if I had my suit. But I could have waded in up to my knees, just for the experience of being in the Pacific on this side of the globe.

Jill sat demurely in the sand while I ventured out to the water. I thought of the Victorian woman in the painting who strolled along the beach in a cotton gown that fell to her ankles. I imagined I was she and stooped to pick up a broken shell.

The warm salt water rushed over my bare feet, as a wave tumbled to shore. I waded out a little deeper and wedged my feet into the sand. Hundreds of swimmers and splashers, along with a few body surfers, frolicked in the sparkling surf, their voices mixing with the crashing sounds of the waves. At the spot where the long sidewalk edged the sandy beach, dozens of tall star pine trees anchored themselves into the sand the way I planned to anchor myself into the sand.

This might be "Manly" beach, but I'm having a very "womanly" moment right now. I smiled at the beauty all around me and twisted my feet deeper into the soft sand.

Just then a loud siren sounded from the shore. Everyone looked around to see what was going on. A voice boomed over the loudspeaker. "Everyone out of the water. We've had a shark sighting. This is not a drill!"

I never knew I could run so fast in sand.

I wasn't the only one who kicked into high gear. The water emptied in seconds. Everyone stood and stared out to sea. Three of the Manly lifeguards jumped in a motorized raft and entered the water. As the crowd of stunned beachgoers watched, the raft headed out to where several surfers had been paddling on their boards, waiting for the waves to pick up.

"I saw it," a woman next to us said. "Did you see? The fin was sticking out of the water."

We all squinted and tried to make out what was going on as the lifeguards motored in a wide circle. One of them motioned to shore, and another raft was launched with three more lifeguards.

"Something is definitely out there," a guy said, moving closer to the shore.

"It's no small wonder, really," said a short woman who stepped up next to us. She was smoking a cigarette with quick, short puffs and wore a bikini even though she had to be at least sixty. "You know they keep sharks in the Oceanworld aquarium just the other side of the wharf in Manly Cove."

"Really?" Jill said, as if trying to make polite conversation yet keeping her eyes glued on the water.

"That's right. You can get in the tank and swim with the sharks, if you like. But swimming out here, in the ocean, you don't know what you might meet up with."

As one great audience we all were standing, inching closer to the water to see what was going on. Everyone spouted opinions and impressions of what was seen out there.

With both rafts motoring in a circle, we watched while one of the lifeguards threw a rope into the water the way a cowboy would toss a lasso.

"They're not going to catch it like that!" someone exclaimed. "That shark will eat them alive."

"It's not a shark," another viewer said. "It's a person."

Everyone in earshot of that observation gasped and strained even harder to see what the lifeguards were now pulling to shore.

"They wouldn't haul a body in like that," someone said. "It has to be a fish. Dolphin, maybe. It's big, whatever it is. Look, isn't that a fin sticking up? Could be a shark, after all. Wouldn't be the first time here. Ah, wait. No worries. It's a log!"

A collective sigh rippled along the shoreline as everyone saw that the Manly lifeguards had bravely lassoed a log with a finlike branch sticking out the topside. Some people laughed; some just looked relieved. A few joked loudly enough so the rest of us could hear.

"They better throw it back in where they got it!" the woman next to us said, rubbing her cigarette stub into the sand. "Otherwise the Greenies will be all over them for disrupting the natural habitat of floating logs."

I was amazed how everyone entered into the conversation and joked around, as if we had all come to the beach that day as one big group. No one seemed to be taking himself or the situation too seriously. I felt like we were at a grand neighborhood picnic.

When people returned to the water, Jill joined them. I watched her step right in, kicking playfully at the waves. I pulled out my camera and took a couple of pictures of her.

Beyond Jill rolled blue, blue ocean for thousands of miles. I thought of my home at the other end of that blue. I missed Skyler; she would love this beach. She would love the "everybody's on vacation" feel of this town and these people. Tony would love it here, too. I wondered if the three of us would ever visit a place like this together, or were our family travel days over?

Using my sweater as a pillow, I lay back and felt the powerful sun on my face. This was a good day. This was a good place to be. I thought of the hundreds of trips to the beach I'd taken at home in California. Those treks always meant packing an ice chest, towels, blankets, and umbrellas. Today we had taken a bus and a ferry to the beach, and here I was in my "Sunday clothes" enjoying the beach with nothing more than a sweater for a pillow. My life definitely had become simplified since we moved here.

A contented smile traipsed across my lips. I wondered if moving into the minimalist apartment had been the first step in learning how to live comfortably with less.

"You look relaxed." Jill stood next to me and playfully sprinkled the last of the salt water that clung to her fingers.

"I am. Hey, is it raining?"

"Just sprinkling."

"How was the water?"

"Shark free and log free. Very nice. Wish we had brought our togs."

"Our what?"

"That's what they call swimsuits here. Our bathing togs."

"I'm sure you could go buy a new one in any of those surf shops we walked past."

"Yeah, I saw a lime green bikini in the window of one shop that I thought might work for me."

I sat up. "Let's do it, Jill. Let's buy a couple of bikinis. Lime green ones. Who cares? Nobody knows us here. When are we ever going to be on this beach again?"

Jill laughed. "My bikini days ended after my third child."

"Who cares? You saw that woman who was standing with us during the shark roundup. And look at that lady over there." I nodded toward a woman who was larger than either Jill or I was. She had on a bikini top and a pair of shorts that covered most of her large rear but didn't stop her belly from hanging over.

"Oh, the peer pressure of it all!" Jill pretended to bite her thumbnail.

"We'll buy cover-ups and stay covered up except when we're in the water. What do you think?"

"You're serious."

"Yes, of course I'm serious. Come on, we'll never be eighteen again, but we can pretend we are for one afternoon while we swim at Manly Beach. What do you say? We might even get a second look from one of those Manly lifeguards."

"Oh, we'll get a second look, all right," Jill said under her breath. "I can almost guarantee you that."

Breezing through several surf shops near the shore, we quickly found that the sizes they carried in swimwear catered to a crowd that was at least thirty years our junior. The first store we went into looked promising because they had such a wide selection on a rack in the back. A sale clerk asked if she could help, and we guessed at the sizes we each needed. She pulled a pink bikini off the rack and handed it to Jill. It was at least two sizes smaller than what Jill needed and three sizes smaller than what I estimated I needed.

"So sorry," the salesclerk said. "That's the largest size we carry."

"Come on." I pulled Jill out of the store. "Shopping for bathing suits is rarely a good idea. In a beach town like this with a strip of fashionable shops, it's a really bad idea."

"They have no idea, do they?" she said, fanning herself. "She had to be all of what? Nineteen, maybe? I doubt she's ever weighed more than a hundred pounds in her life. Young and thin and beautiful. They think they rule the world."

"I know. She's probably a cheerleader, too."

Jill paused and then gave me a glinty-eyed look. "Oh, that was low, Salerno!"

That's when I remembered that Jill had been a cheerleader.

I wasn't referring to her; the words had just bumbled out of my mouth.

"Sorry!" I pinched my fingers together and pretended to zip my mouth closed.

"You don't have to zip it, Kathy. I'm way beyond being offended. Let's go do something else." Jill pushed back her hair and flapped the collar of her blouse in an effort to cool off.

"We can still go back and enjoy the beach. Or if you want, we can shop like we did yesterday. That was fun. They have a lot of souvenir shops around here with cute stuff other than clothes."

Jill fanned her rosy face. "I have to stick with my own rule on this one."

"What's that?"

"Shop till you drop or a hot flash makes you stop."

Seventeen

I laughed at Jill's hot flash joke as we walked back toward Manly Beach, where more balmy hours of the day awaited us.

Looking over her shoulder, Jill said, "Is that an ice cream shop?"

"Comfort food?"

"You know it."

I led the way. "American comfort food beats Vegemite any day."

We bought waffle cones with single scoops and strolled along the extended walkway that lined the immense stretch of beach.

"We could be skinny again if we wanted to be," Jill said.

"Speak for yourself. I never was skinny."

"I'm more concerned about staying healthy than getting skinny."

We agreed and reviewed all the reasons healthy was better

than skinny. Then we compared our health problems, scar tissue, and choices of vitamins and agreed that, when it came to stretch marks, we were powerless.

"Mine are all on my thighs," I said.

"My belly is atrocious," Jill said. "I can't believe you almost talked me into putting on a bikini and exposing my stomach to the public. The notion was liberating for a few minutes, but maybe that little princess was right; bikinis shouldn't be sold in mama-sizes."

We spent the rest of the afternoon enjoying the sand, sun, and soft ocean breeze. For dinner we bought fish and chips at a take-away place across from the beach and ate on the cement sea wall with our feet hanging over the edge.

"Before we board the ferry," I said. "I have to buy one thing, if you don't mind shopping with me for this souvenir."

"Sure," Jill said. "Are you going to buy one of those Manly Beach hats after all?"

"No." I opened the door for her to a small shop. "I think you and I need matching Manly Beach towels."

I got mine in yellow. Jill picked blue. We also bought some postcards and floaty pens that showed a Manly ferry rolling back and forth in the harbor every time the pen was tilted.

Then Jill found the best souvenir of the trip. It was a long stick with a trigger handle. On the top of the stick was a plastic shark. Every time the trigger was activated, the shark opened its mouth and snapped its plastic teeth. We bought matching sharks, too.

"So, what do you want to do tomorrow?" Jill asked while we waited in line to board our return ferry. "We don't have all day since our flight goes out at seven that night. I wish now we had arranged to stay longer. There's so much more to see here."

"I know. I'd like to go to the Blue Mountains. Did you see that brochure?"

"Is that where the Three Sisters are? Those three big rock formations?"

"That's right," said an older man standing near us. His Australian accent sounded as if he had been gargling with gravel. "The Blue Mountains are two hours from here. You should see some of the outback while you're here. Cleve's Bush Walkers put on a fine tour. It's an all-day tour, though."

"Thanks," Jill said. "I don't think we'll have enough time on this trip."

"Well, you remember Cleve's Bush Walkers then for your next visit. They'll show you the sights and fix you up with some lizard for lunch."

"Lizard?" Jill repeated.

"Goanna lizards are 'bout this long. Skewer it right on a stick over an open fire, and you've got yourself a meal. Cleve catches 'em and cooks up enough for the entire tour group."

"And tourists actually eat… " Jill could barely say the word, "…lizard?"

"Aww, no worries. Goanna lizard's not so bad. The way Cleve sautés it, you'll say it tastes like chicken."

I noticed that Jill had moved away from the helpful man.

"What's wrong, Jill? Are you not fond of lizards?"

She lowered her chin and looked at me hard without answering. That's when I knew I had her.

"So, would you say that you're not fond of lizards, or would you say the way you feel about lizards is similar to the way I feel about bats?"

"Kathy, please." She turned away from the guy in line and lowered her voice. "I beg you. Grace me on this one, will you?

I'll let you slide with the nasty cheerleader comment, but I can't talk about lizards." Her voice was so low she only mouthed the last two words.

"No worries." I grinned. "Your secret is safe with me."

Our source of outback lore had taken up with some Asian tourists, leaving Jill and me to make a dash for it once the next ferry started to board passengers. We scrambled up to the top deck so we could have prime seats to watch the dramatic approach into Sydney Harbor. The sun was beginning its fading act, slipping behind the landscape of tall buildings as the city lights were coming on. I thought it strange to watch a sunset that wasn't dipping into the Pacific. Here, the sun rose out of the ocean.

"Look." Jill pointed to the star-studded sky. "The Southern Cross. Did you recognize it?"

I'd never seen the Southern Cross. I stared at the night sky. Even the stars looked different in the lower half of the hemisphere.

Down under. Backwards. Upside down. Everything is different in this place.

"What a gorgeous night," Jill said.

We wrapped our new beach towels around our shoulders for warmth and watched the harbor bridge come into view. The bridge's lights, along with the lights coming from the Opera House on the far left, sparkled dramatically over the calm, teal waters that were fading to black.

"So, what are we going to do tomorrow?" Jill asked.

"Can it involve an animal?"

Jill didn't look amused. "What kind of animal?"

Imitating the voice of the man in line, I said, "No worries, mate. I'm not talking about seeing a…" I mouthed the word *lizard.* "How about finding us a real, live kangaroo?"

"Yes, great idea," Jill said. "We have to pet a koala bear while we're here, too. I know they have a wildlife park somewhere, and a zoo."

We settled back in our Manly Beach towels as the ferry approached the dock. This had been a fine day.

To make our fine day complete, upon returning to the hotel, we ordered room service and checked out a video from the hotel collection of Australian films. I was all set for *Crocodile Dundee*, but keeping Jill's lizard and possible additional reptile phobias in mind, I agreed to a documentary on Ayers Rock.

However, as soon as we ate, we fell asleep. So much for showing documentaries at a slumber party.

When the phone rang at seven with our morning wake-up call, we both rolled over and moaned that we wanted to sleep some more.

Jill got up before I did. Her turn in the shower gave me a chance to wake slowly. As I did, I thought of how, for so many years, my morning prayer had been along the lines of, "Please let my day go smoothly." It struck me that such a prayer always came with the assumption that the day was "my" day, and the schedule was "my" schedule. All I was asking for was God's nod of approval on my agenda, as if He were my supervisor. Figuring out life was up to me. I never invited His rearranging. Rarely did I enter into the ebb and flow of speaking and listening, which I knew was essential for any relationship, if it was to grow.

Reaching for the devotional I'd brought with me, I read the verse for that day. I was hoping the verse would speak to me the same way the Ephesians verse had started me thinking about extravagant love.

Today the verses were from Lamentations 3. It wasn't a book of the Bible I'd turned to often, but I recognized the passage. "The unfailing love of the LORD never ends!... Great is his faithfulness; his mercies begin afresh each day."

Sitting up in bed, I whispered humbly to the Great God of this universe, the God who rules all that is visible and invisible, upside-down and right side up, that I'd rather experience His extravagant love and mercy every day than to receive the check-off mark I'd been asking for all these years. I pictured myself laying aside my day and waiting for Him to offer His day to me as a gift.

When Jill stepped out of the bathroom I smiled. "Do you want to hear a great verse for us for today?" She sat on the edge of her bed towel drying her hair while I read the Lamentations verse to her.

Stopping abruptly, Jill looked at me. "There's more to that chapter, you know." She pulled out her journal and flipped to one of the pages in the middle. "These verses were sent to me in a card right after Ray died, and they hit me so hard it was as if I couldn't swallow them. I wrote them here because I knew that one day I'd be able to read them, and they wouldn't make me choke."

She looked down at her journal and then back at me, as if she was looking for encouragement before taking a leap.

"Would you like me to read it?"

"No, I can do this." Jill's voice was tight as she read. "'I will never forget this awful time, as I grieve over my loss. Yet I still dare to hope when I remember this: The unfailing love of the LORD never ends! By his mercies we have been kept from complete destruction. Great is his faithfulness; his mercies begin afresh each day.... For the Lord does not abandon anyone forever. Though he brings grief, he also shows compassion according to the greatness of his unfailing love. For he does not enjoy hurting people or causing them sorrow.... Can anything happen without the Lord's permission?'"

I watched Jill's expression as she tried to swallow the strong words. She turned to me with a hopeful smile. "It's taken me two years to believe that God didn't utterly abandon me. He does show compassion. It's taken me this long to begin to believe that."

"I admire you so much, Jill."

"I don't know if I'm to be admired. I still have a hard time with the last part of that passage. If nothing happens without the Lord's permission, then why would such a compassionate God give permission for Ray to die? It doesn't make sense to me. I keep looking for a reason, but there isn't any."

I still didn't know how Ray had died, so I felt inadequate to offer any suggestions. Over the years I'd heard plenty of answers to that question from friends at church, but here, in this place of upside down, none of those reasons seemed to fit.

"Do you think God is fair?" Jill asked.

I wasn't sure how to answer that. What came out of my mouth was, "He must not be."

Jill looked surprised.

"I mean, I've never done anything to deserve the love and mercy He gives me each day. If He were fair, I'd be condemned."

Jill looked down at her hands for a long pause. "I guess it does work both ways, doesn't it? That is, if there's a balance in life the same way there is in art, we don't deserve all the good things He gives us, do we?"

"I know I don't."

"And His love is pretty generous, when you think of all the things that could go wrong every day."

"I happen to have a verse about that." I turned to the Ephesians passage I liked so much. "Tell me what you think of this. 'Mostly what God does is love you. Keep company with him and learn a life of love. Observe how Christ loved us. His love was not cautious but extravagant. He didn't love in order to get something from us but to give everything of himself to us. Love like that.'"

"'Not cautious but extravagant,'" Jill repeated. "That's hard to do after you've been hurt deeply."

I nodded even though I knew I'd never experienced the same deep wound that Jill had.

"Would it be okay if I copied that verse?"

"Sure." I handed her the devotional book and headed for the shower. Turning at the bathroom door, I said, "I still believe what I said to you the day we had tea at my house. You are not invisible. To other people or to God. You are very much alive, Jill."

Her smile broke the somber cloud she had been sitting under. "Thanks, Kathy."

While I showered and finished dressing and packing up, Jill went to gather information from the concierge about where we could find a "real, live kangaroo." The option she chose was a wildlife park outside the city, not far from the Olympic stadium.

Jill and I rented a car, this time directly from the hotel. The vehicle was equipped with a satellite navigational system that saved us from getting lost and driving around in circles.

The automated voice on the directional system said, "Turn right five hundred meters ahead," and we turned right. It was a wonderful thing.

We pulled into the Olympic Park and drove around looking at the arenas. Jill found a parking place, and we walked to the main square. Seeing the structure where the Olympic torch for the 2000 games had burned so brightly choked me up. The huge Olympic "cauldron," as they called it, was now a spectacular fountain at the center of a park surrounded by leafy fig trees. What got to me was the awareness that I was standing in a place where history had been made.

Jill was even more affected by the fountain. When I looked at her, tears were streaming down her cheeks.

"I'm sorry I keep crying all the time."

"That's okay."

"It's just that Ray came here. For the 2000 games. He and I were supposed to come for four days, but I had a sinus infection that went into my ears. I was afraid if I got on a plane my eardrums would burst. So Ray came by himself and had a wonderful time without me."

She drew in a wobbly breath. "I never knew I'd regret losing four days with him out of the thousands we spent together. If I had it to do over, I would have chanced the burst eardrums."

I paused a moment. "No, you probably wouldn't have."

Jill looked at me, surprised for the second time that morning by my quiet irreverence to her lament.

"I mean, maybe you would have done things differently, if given the chance. But, really, Jill, you made the best decision at that time based on the circumstances."

She adjusted her sunglasses. "You're right. When you think you have all the time in the world with someone, you focus more on yourself than on him."

We walked around the fountain in silence, reading the names of the athletes who had received medals at the 2000 games etched in the pavement.

"Thank you," Jill said as we got back in the car.

"For what?"

"For telling me what I needed to hear. It's as if all these small doors in my heart keep opening and the closed-up hurt and tears come pouring out. You must be sick of this by now."

"Not yet."

"The only good is that each time one of those doors opens, I feel as if I'm healing. You keep giving me truth, Kathy, and I need that. When I'm left to my own imagination, I tell myself all kinds of things. Not everything I tell myself is true."

"We all do that. More than once you've given me truth, you know."

"All I know is that having you here, right now during this time in my life, feels like God sent an extravagant gift to me. I mean, when I think about it, he brought you here all the way from my grandpa's orange grove!"

"So what you're saying is that you see me as a big fruit, is that it?"

Jill chuckled.

I tried to honor the seriousness of her observation. What I intended to say was, "I've benefited greatly from your friendship, too, you know." But what came out was, "I've bene-fruited from your friendship, too, you know."

That's when we both cracked up.

"We make quite a pear," Jill said between her laughter bubbles. "Get it? Pair? Pear?"

It took a few minutes for us to compose ourselves before Jill started the engine. I punched in the wildlife park's address on the keyboard for the directional system, and a map with a red line showed up on the screen. We dabbed away our giggle-tears, and before long found ourselves winding through a hilly canyon that we both said reminded us of Trabuco Canyon in California. The eucalyptus trees were what made the connection for me.

The park wasn't large, and only a few visitors strolled around. But our timing was perfect because we arrived five minutes before the feeding of the koalas. The fuzzy, gray fur balls draped themselves in the most humorous poses over a dozen tree stands. We stood only a few feet away from the open area and watched the sluggish snuggle bears while they did absolutely nothing but try to keep from falling off their posts.

A park guide entered the center area with switches of fresh eucalyptus. One of the eight koala bears opened his eyes long enough to pay attention to what was happening.

"Come here, then, Victor." She reached for the koala by the arms and pulled him toward her the way I'd seen a chimpanzee reach for a long-armed baby chimp. The guide positioned Victor on the railing, handed him a sprig of eucalyptus leaves, and filled the visitors in on the facts about koalas. The one bit of information that everyone laughed at was how the average koala sleeps for eighteen hours a day.

"Think about that the next time your teenager doesn't want to get out of bed on a Saturday."

We were invited to come close and have our pictures taken with Victor. Jill pulled out her camera and snapped a shot of me with my arm around the oblivious fellow while he munched on leaves with his eyes half shut. I couldn't believe how soft he was. I'd heard a mom call her little girl a "cuddly koala" on one of our earlier bus rides, and now that phrase had more meaning. This little guy was irresistibly snuggly.

Jill took her turn for the picture. I snapped three from different angles. A startling sound made us stop and look around.

"What was that?" I asked.

"Kookaburra," the park guide said. "It's a bird with a loud call."

"Sounds like a donkey," Jill said.

"You'll find the kookaburras in the aviary by going left on the trail through the park."

"What about the kangaroos?" I asked.

"Keep to the right on the trail."

We set off and found a sign at the trails' intersection. Arrows pointed to our options of animals to visit. I read the list aloud. "Wallabies, dingoes, emus, wallaroos, wombats...here we are. Grey kangaroos. This direction."

"This seems unreal, doesn't it?" Jill asked.

"What do you mean?"

"All these animals! It's hard to believe they're real."

"You just touched a koala bear," I said.

"I know. But the sign could point us to the unicorn pen, and I'd believe there was such a thing as a unicorn."

I knew I'd feel the same way the moment I saw a real, live kangaroo up close. Kangaroos always seemed mythical to me. I didn't know if it was the concept of the built-in front pocket, which any mother could make good use of, or if it was the way they hopped. All I knew was that, according to the sign, if we stayed on this path, we would come face-to-face with a real, live kangaroo.

Eighteen

A fence and a low gate with a simple latch enclosed the kangaroo area at the wildlife park. Jill lifted the latch, and we entered a dirt area that was partially shaded. To my delight, a kangaroo about two feet tall came hopping over.

I chortled. "It's a kangaroo!"

"What were you expecting?"

"It's hopping! Look! It's a hopping kangaroo."

"That's what they do, Kathy."

"I know, but this is my unicorn, like you were just saying. I can't believe it's real and that they let us come into this area with them. Hello, little guy. You are so cute. You know I have food, don't you?"

When we bought our entry tickets to the park, we had also purchased two bags labeled "kangaroo food." I opened my bag and looked inside to see what kangaroos liked to eat.

"Cheerios? Jill, look! The kangaroo food is Cheerios! Do you know how much I've missed Cheerios since we left California? I can't believe the kangaroos get to eat Cheerios!"

"Maybe it isn't really Cheerios." Jill sniffed the contents of her kangaroo food bag. "Maybe it just looks like Cheerios."

"It smells like Cheerios." I held a small amount in my hand and smelled the round o's.

"Kathy, you're not going to eat them, are you?"

"Why not? They're Cheerios."

"You don't know that. Not for sure."

My mouth was just an inch from my handful of Cheerios. My tongue slid over my lower lip, oh so willing to connect with one of the tiny o's.

"Kathy, don't do it!" Jill squealed. "You should see yourself! You look so funny. Even if those are Cheerios, you don't know where those little o's have been."

I pulled back my tongue. "You're right."

While we carried on our Cheerios debate, the kangaroos in the open area were slowly hopping toward us. I looked down, and one fellow was checking around my feet for any dropped treats.

"Put some in your hand, and see if he'll eat out of your palm." Jill reached for the camera.

"What if he bites the hand that feeds him?"

"Then I'll take a nice close-up shot for the insurance claim."

"I don't see you sticking your hand out here."

"Somebody has to take the pictures."

The patient little kangaroo looked up at me with the most adorable doe eyes I'd ever seen. The long, innocent lashes seemed to be batting at me, pleading for me to share my precious Cheerios.

"Hello," I said to the unafraid kangaroo. "Or should I say, g'day?"

He rose to his full height and came up to my hip.

"Are you hungry? These are Cheerios, you know. Do you like Cheerios?"

"They're not Cheerios," Jill said.

"Don't listen to her. I know Cheerios when I see them. And you are so cute I'm going to share my Cheerios with you. Here."

He put out his small paws so that they held steady my hand. With a flick of his long, dry tongue, this real, live kangaroo ate out of my hand.

I laughed with glee. "His tongue tickles! Look at him! He is so adorable! I want to take him home with me!"

Another kangaroo rose from the shade and hopped over on feet the size of baby-sized water skis. I laughed again. I couldn't help it. These guys were irresistible. Their ears stood straight up, flicking, listening, picking up every sound.

The other kangaroo joined the littler one, and the two of them peaceably ate together from my hand.

"Here you go. Hang on. Let me get some more. Jill, you have to feed one of them. They are so sweet."

"I'll feed this one," she said, as a larger kangaroo came bounding our way. It was about three feet away when Jill let out a soft squeal. "Kathy, look! This one has a baby. In her pocket!"

I thought I was going to cry, I was so happy. The image of that mama kangaroo hopping over to us and standing mere inches away with her little joey popping out of her pouch had to be one of the most amazing things I'd ever seen.

Jill giggled.

I was right with her. "I can't believe you're real," I said to the kangaroos. It was as if a fairy tale had come true before my eyes.

Jill's infectious laughter filled the air. The unafraid kangaroos came closer, their big eyes looking up at us with curious blinks. The joey stuck one arm out of his mama's pouch, then the other, and twisted around, as if trying to look up into our faces. The first kangaroo rested his tiny paw on my leg, the way a toddler reaches to feel the security of his mother beside him.

The delight of that moment imbedded itself in my mind as sweetly and as permanently as the memory of my first kiss.

I touched the soft fur of the steady fellow and whispered, "You're real."

Much later that same night when I arrived home, Tony said he wanted to hear all about our trip. My conversation kept returning to the kangaroos.

"You really liked those magical marsupials, didn't you? Or was it the Cheerios you were really crazy about?"

I threw a pillow at him. "You would have been proud of me. I didn't eat any of the kanga food. I thought about it, but I didn't snatch a single *o*. I couldn't once I saw those darling faces with those big eyes looking up at me." I demonstrated with my best kangaroo expression.

Tony smiled. "I love it when you're like this."

"Like what?"

"Full of life. Happy."

"Do you really want to see me full of life? Then let's go to Australia. You and me. What do you think?" I snuggled up to Tony.

"You just want to go back and see your kangaroo pals."

"Yes, and other parts of the country. The concierge at the hotel told us we needed to come back in the winter to go skiing in the south. He said the season opens in June. Isn't that crazy? Skiing in July? That's too late for us, though, because we'll be back in California by then."

"Maybe," Tony said.

"What do you mean *maybe*?" I watched his expression closely to make sure he wasn't joking around.

"I put my name in today for another project. It doesn't mean I'll get it, and it doesn't mean I'll take it if it's offered. We had a big meeting this morning. Walter announced his next production and gave all of us a chance to put in for specific positions before the studio goes public with the project."

"What's the film?"

Tony smiled but kept his lips sealed. I knew that meant that if he told me he would have to kill me. Insiders are very loyal in his industry when it comes to not releasing information on a film before the studio is ready to issue a press release. Anyone who slips and divulges information is treated like an infidel and is kept out of the loop on further industry disclosures.

"What do you think?" Tony asked.

"If you have the chance to take the job and you really want it, then take it, Tony."

"Are you sure?"

"Yes."

"I know it was hard for you when we first got here. You've done a great job of making the best of it. I don't want to put too much of a strain on you."

"You're not. I'm okay with staying. Really."

Tony scratched the back of his neck and looked at me as if to say, *Who are you and what have you done with the wife I brought over here with me?*

"I thought you wouldn't like the idea because it would

mean staying here longer, and if you're eager to go back to school, it could slow down that process."

"It might. Or I might be able to take classes here. I don't know. I'm not worried about that right now, Tony. What matters the most to me is that you have a chance to pursue some of your dreams. My turn will come."

Something inside of me felt that was true. That's the only way to describe what I was feeling. I didn't know how to express it. In my heart, I knew that God was extravagant with His love and His gifts to His children. I also knew that this was a time for me to be extravagant with my husband by giving him all the freedom he needed to pursue this next opportunity. It felt right.

Tony didn't seem to know what to say, but it didn't matter. What followed were lots of mushy kisses and not a lot of words.

On Wednesday, Jill and I met at the Chocolate Fish at our usual table. Tracey brought a whole plate of chocolate fish and pulled up a chair, eager to hear all our stories about Sydney. Jill presented Tracey with one of our little squeaking kangaroos. Tracey laughed and said she would let him ride around on the dashboard of Beatrice.

"Or better yet," Tracey said, "how about if I manage some sort of pouch on the front of Beatrice? We could tuck this little joey in the pocket on the grille."

I didn't doubt that Tracey might try such a setup just to watch our reactions.

"I'm so glad you're getting out and getting on with your life, Jill. It's a good thing. I'm sure you know that."

Jill nodded. "I know. I can't believe how much has changed for me in the past few weeks."

"It's ever since *she* showed up." Tracey grinned and pretended to shield her mouth, as if I couldn't hear her.

"I'm sitting right here, you know."

"I know. And I hope you know how great it is that you showed up when you did. Which reminds me, what are you two doing Friday night?"

Jill and I both said we had no plans.

"Then what do you think of the three of us having a girls' night out? I thought we could go to the movies."

"Sounds fun."

"Good. We have a plan. Now, I'd love to sit here another hour, but there's no telling what state the kitchen has gotten into while I've been chatting." Tracey started walking away and added, "I'll pick you up in Bea around six-thirty on Friday. And dress like you mean it."

Jill and I swapped glances that said we weren't sure what Tracey's last line meant. All I knew was that I had a ton of laundry to do. I told Jill, "I've been waiting for another sunny day, so I can hang the clothes outside instead of in the bathtub. I'm beginning to miss having a clothes dryer more than I thought I would."

"More than Cheerios?" Jill asked.

"Yes, more than Cheerios."

"What else do you miss?"

"A little bit of everything, but nothing so much that I can't wait to go back." I was about to tell Jill about the possibility of Tony's extended assignment, but for some reason it seemed better to wait until the possibility was stronger. I could see the two of us making plans to do something four months from now, and then, if Tony didn't get the job, it would feel like the disastrous bathing suit shopping experience. It seemed better to keep quiet until I could talk confidently about staying.

"You know what I realized the other day? I miss teaching," Jill said.

"You do?"

"I really do. I haven't taught for the past few years, but after you were so kind as to play the role of the interested student at the art museum in Sydney, I've been thinking about how much I love it."

"I wasn't playing the role of the interested student. I was interested. I'm sure I gave you a hard time about it, but, Jill, you're a great teacher. I learned so much. You have such a freshness and passion in the way you explain everything."

"I forgot I had that passion."

"Well, the passion is definitely back. You should do something about it."

Jill looked out the window at the water and drew in a deep breath, as if she were trying to breathe in the fresh, salty air. I realized this was the same profile I'd seen the day we met. But this time, instead of tears on her face, I saw a chin-up look of determination.

"Maybe this is the treasure you're holding in your hand," I suggested, thinking of the painting we had enjoyed together in Sydney.

Jill swished her lips back and forth the way she did when she was contemplating something. "No," she said after a moment. "This isn't it. Feeling the passion for teaching is a good thing, but this isn't the treasure I hold in my hand."

"Do you know what it is?"

"Not yet."

"I almost forgot." I reached into my purse and pulled out a card-sized envelope. "It's not exactly a treasure by any means, but I do have a little something for you. Here."

Jill looked at the envelope. "You're not going to believe this, but I have a card for you, too."

We exchanged envelopes, and I opened mine first. On the front of the homemade card Jill had doodled an adorable mama kangaroo. She had bright pink lips; long, flippy eyelashes; and a broad Manly Beach hat on her head. In her pouch was a box of tissues.

Inside Jill had written, "Thanks for showing up when you did, Kathy. You have no idea how much I appreciate you. I have thanked God a million times for you and the sunshine of your friendship. If you ever need me for anything, just say the word, and I'll be there in one big kangaroo hop."

"I love it, Jill. Thank you." I flipped back to the kangaroo doodle on the front and smiled. "This is so cute."

"I considered adding Cheerios," Jill said dryly. "But I was afraid you'd try to lick them off the paper."

"Very funny."

As Jill opened my envelope, I felt compelled to apologize. "Now remember, I'm not an artist like you."

"I'm not an artist," Jill said quickly.

"Yes, you are! Look at this. I could never draw like this."

"I'm a doodler, Kathy. Not an artist."

"Doodling is art."

She pulled my card out of the envelope. "And so is this! How fun! The feathers!"

"You recognize them?"

"Of course. Although they did look a little more artsy in your hair than here on paper."

"That's because I'm not an artist. Not even a doodler."

Jill opened the card and read my one-liner aloud. "'Sisterchicks of a feather sip lattes together!' How perfect!"

"I hope I managed to glue the two feathers at the right median and interpose the best ratio balance for the canvas."

Jill cracked up. "You were listening."

"Told you I was. If an art appreciation class doesn't open up for you to teach, I think you should consider leading art appreciation tours. I'd be the first to sign up."

"Now that sounds like fun. How about art tours to Paris? They have that big Louvre, you know." Her twinkling-eyed expression made it clear that she thought she was flinging out the wildest of all possibilities.

I wasn't ready to scale it down. "Why not? You have the time, the expertise, and you love to travel. There's no reason you shouldn't lead art appreciation tours to Paris."

Jill looked as if a whirlwind of possibilities was about to sweep her up and transport her to an exotic locale.

I knew that feeling.

Nineteen

Friday morning I asked Tony if he had heard anything new on the job opening. He said, "Mad Dog thinks they hit a judder bar with the finances. Nothing new. Happens all the time."

"Wait. What did you say? They hit a what?"

Tony thought back on what he had said. "Oh, a judder bar."

"And what is a judder bar?"

Tony smiled and wheeled his bike toward the door. "Haven't you heard that one around here yet? That's what the guys at work call a speed bump. I gotta go, Kath. I love you."

I kissed him as he flew out the door and called out, "Make sure you don't hit any judder bars!"

I had some wet laundry ready to hang on the line, and the morning sunshine motivated me to jump on the chore. The act of standing and stretching my arms over my head to fasten sheets and shirts and even my underwear to the clothesline had become a small act of worship. I loved the way the soft breezes would come and make the clothes move. My pj's danced without music. In a funny little way, I envied them.

Tony called my cell phone around four o'clock, and I reminded him that I'd made plans to go to the movies with Tracey and Jill that night.

"Maybe you and Mad Dog can do something after work," I suggested.

"No can do. Mad Dog has a blind date."

"A blind date? With whom?"

Tony paused. "If he knew, it wouldn't be a blind date, now would it?"

"Tell him I hope it goes well."

"Yeah, well, if it doesn't go well, I'm his out."

"What do you mean?"

"If he wants an excuse to leave, he's going to dial my cell and hang up. I'm supposed to call him back and make it sound like he has to come to the studio immediately."

"I can't believe you guys are doing that! How do you think the poor woman is going to feel?"

Tony hesitated again, as if I'd missed the obvious. "Have you forgotten who we're talking about here? This is Mad Dog. What woman wouldn't thank me for making the call?"

"Tony!"

"Don't worry. Mad Dog is standing right here. I'm just giving him a hard time. You should see the guy. He's as nervous as a cat. A Mad Cat."

In the background I heard a loud "meow!"

"What are you planning to do, then? Are you going to come home and wait for Mad Dog's call or stay there at work?"

"I think I'll stay here. Don't worry about me. I have plenty to do."

"Okay. I'll see you when I get back."

Tony's voice took on an ethereal quality as he added, "I hope you and your friends have the time of your life during this time of your life."

He was mocking Tracey's inspirational line, but I didn't care. I kind of liked being in his lineup of friends that he could tease. It was a good place for our marriage to be.

Beatrice, the Blazing Bumble Bee, pulled up in the gravel driveway at precisely 6:35, and I was ready to go. Jill and Tracey looked gorgeous. Both of them had done their hair and makeup with a little more pizzazz than usual. Jill had on a lime green sweater set with the sleeves pushed up and a row of beaded bracelets on her forearm. She looked fresh and cute.

"I don't think I dressed up enough." I looked at my knit shirt, jeans, and athletic shoes.

"We have time, if you want to make a quick change," Tracey said. "It's up to you."

"I'll be right back." Dashing inside, I remembered that Tracey had told us to dress like we meant it. I wasn't sure on Wednesday what that meant, and now I wasn't sure what combination in my wardrobe would fit that description. Going for a pair of sandals instead of the running shoes was a good first step. The jeans were okay, but I dressed them up with a crisp white blouse that I'd ironed for the trip to Sydney and then hadn't packed. One of the plusses of having dark hair and eyes was that anytime I wore white, I looked like I'd cleaned up. The opal earrings and necklace I bought in Sydney were a quick add-on, and I was out the door.

"Classy," Jill said, when I slid in the front seat next to her.

"That's a great look on you," Tracey agreed. "Love the earrings."

"Thanks. Sorry to keep you waiting."

"No worries. We have time." Tracey eased Bea out of the driveway and down the road.

We chatted like a box of budgies, which I'd learned meant we sounded like a bunch of cheerful, twittering birds. When Tracey approached the Embassy Theatre, I knew where we were. That was a Wellington first for me.

"Are you two popcorn eaters?" Tracey asked. "Or should we go out for Pavlova afterward?"

I didn't know what Pavlova was, but popcorn seemed mandatory for a girls' night out at the movies.

"We're getting it with extra butter, of course," Tracey said, as we stepped in line at the concession stand. "And three large diet soft drinks to cancel the effects of the extra butter."

The three of us were chuckling at the universal female dieting logic, when a man came up behind Jill and said, "If you're the lady in green, I'm the man in black."

We all turned and I nearly shrieked. "Mad Dog!"

He stumbled back half a step on the plush carpet. "Kathleen, what are you doing here?"

"Mad Dog?" Jill echoed.

"Hallo!" Tracey said.

I'd never seen Mad Dog look so stunned. He even took off his cap and greeted Jill with reverence.

Jill barely moved.

Mad Dog nervously glanced at me and then at Tracey. I saw the cell phone looped on his belt buckle, ready to draw.

Regaining his composure, Mad Dog said, "Ahh, just wanted to…yeah. Well. Have a nice evening. Hope you enjoy the show." He looked over the top of my head, and by his expression it was clear that another woman dressed in green had entered the building.

Mad Dog bolted across the lobby, and the three of us watched as a young-looking blonde in a tight emerald green sweater smiled and responded to his pickup line.

"Well, Bob's your uncle," Tracey said. "That was a bit on the awkward side, wasn't it?"

Jill still hadn't said anything.

It was our turn to order. Tracey stepped up to the counter and asked for a tub of buttered popcorn. "Jill, you want anything else?"

"No."

We found three seats near the front, and Jill settled in the middle between Tracey and me. I looked around the beautifully refurbished theater and felt as if we had stepped back in time to an era when viewing a film was a big event and everyone dressed up for the occasion.

I kept glancing at Jill to see if she had snapped out of the haze she slipped into after the less-than-suave encounter with Mad Dog. Obviously more happened in the concession line than Mad Dog mistaking his blind date's identity.

"You know, Jill." Tracey leaned over with the tub of popcorn on her lap. "If you think you might be interested in a blind date yourself one of these days, I have a possibility in mind for you."

"That's okay."

"No, really. This guy has a great personality."

Jill still wasn't smiling. I couldn't tell if Tracey was teasing or really trying to set up Jill.

"He has a great sense of humor, too."

"Not interested."

"His name is—"

"I don't want to know." Jill's freshly manicured fingers covered Tracey's mouth.

"But he has nothing to do with the film industry," Tracey said as the lights dimmed.

"Still not interested."

In one final attempt, Tracey leaned over and said, "He delivers our buns."

That one got Jill. A slight grin inched across her lips. She turned to me. "Will you trade places with me?"

I knew she wasn't serious about trading. I was beginning to catch on to the sarcastic twist in Kiwi humor.

"Come on, Kathy, trade places with me. Please?"

"He has really large buns," Tracey said in an exaggeratedly loud whisper.

Jill reached for a handful of popcorn and told Tracey to "shush" upon threat of being assaulted with the popcorn.

The three of us laughed a lot during the film. Not because the movie was hilarious, but because Tracey kept slipping in more strategic puns. Bun puns, to be precise.

We left the theater feeling euphoric.

"Pavlova anyone?" Tracey asked. "I thought we would go to Sophie's. Have you been there yet, Kathy?"

"No, I take all my dining business to the Chocolate Fish."

"Good answer," Tracey said. "Remind me to give you a chocolate fish next time you're in."

"I'm beginning to feel like a trained seal with all the little fish you keep tossing at me."

Tracey laughed and promised she would cut back on the fish treats. "Either that or you'll have to equip our table with a row of squeaky horns, so I can start entertaining the other guests."

Jill laughed that time, and I felt so happy.

There is nothing as fabulous as the feeling of belonging.

Sophie's turned out to be a small restaurant in the Lambton Quay area. As we entered, Tracey told us that Wellington had more restaurants and cafés per capita than New York City.

"I'm always ready to scout new places to eat," she said, as the three of us took our seats at a table in the corner. "Unless the restaurant is in the wop wops."

"Out in the boonies," Jill translated for me.

"A wop wop would be a great name for a kiddy treat," I said. "It's so fun to say. Wop wops. Wop wops. Try it. Wop wops."

Tracey looked at Jill. "Now I'm the one who wants to change seats. You can sit by the wop-wop woman."

The waitress stepped up to our table, and Tracey said, "Cappuccinos all around?"

"Decaf," I said.

Tracey turned to me as if I'd ordered denture cream. "Decaf? Oh, come on, Kathy, live a little!"

"Okay, regular."

We all laughed some more. The waitress walked away, not at all impressed with our humor.

"Jill," Tracey's expression turned earnest, "I'm glad you bounced back."

Jill nodded.

"It's a new day." Tracey continued her pep talk. I assumed they were talking about the awkward encounter with Mad Dog, but I didn't know if I should enter the conversation. It felt catty to say that I knew he was going on a blind date. What I didn't know was Jill's connection with Mad Dog or why seeing each other had affected them so intensely.

Our cappuccinos came, and we let Tracey order dessert for us since she kept saying Sophie's made the best Pavlova in town. Tracey said she was eager to hear my opinion of the dessert, as an unbiased American. I told her I had nothing to compare it to since, as far as I knew, I'd never had Pavlova.

"Have you told her the story behind it?" Tracey asked Jill.

Jill shook her head so Tracey jumped right in. "Supposedly when the Russian ballerina Anna Pavlova came to New Zealand, a chef created this airy dessert to keep the dancer light on her feet when she performed. The Australians say they created it, but the Kiwis know it came from one of their chefs first."

"So what's in a Pavlova?" I asked.

"It's made of egg whites," Jill said. "Sort of a sweet meringue. Sometimes it has fruit on top; other times it's drizzled with chocolate. I've never had one I didn't like."

The Pavlova looked like a slice of pie, cut in a triangle shape, covered with raspberries, chocolate sauce, and a fat dollop of whipping cream. The texture was light and airy, and the taste was sweet, but not too sugary sweet.

"Two thumbs up," I said after the first bite.

Tracey grinned. "We'll make a Kiwi out of you yet. We did a pretty good job with Jill, don't you think? Oh, there's Susanne! Hallo! Do you two know Susanne?"

"No." We smiled and politely nodded at the young woman who had just entered the restaurant.

"If you don't mind, I'm going to pop over and say hallo. I'll bring her back around to introduce you." Tracey slid out of her seat and met Susanne with Tracey's trademark bright greeting and cheery hug. Instead of returning to the table, the two of them began a head-tilting, much-nodding sort of conversation.

Jill looked down at her unfinished Pavlova and smoothed her finger over the handle of her cappuccino cup. She let out a long sigh and blinked, as if trying to keep back the tears.

"You okay?"

"Kathy, do you know how Ray died?"

"No."

"Do you mean Tony still hasn't said anything to you?"

"No."

"Or Mad Dog?"

"No. I never asked either of them. Like I told you that night in the hotel in Christchurch, if and when you want to tell me, I want to hear. But you don't have to tell me anything, if you don't want to. It won't change my relationship with you one way or the other."

Jill's expression was one of gratitude. "Jackamond is such a small studio. I thought for sure someone would have said something to you by now. I didn't want to be the one to bring it up."

"You don't have to say anything, if you don't want to."

"No, I want you to know. I want to be the one to tell you. I'm ready to talk about it now." Jill lifted her chin, her expression steady. "I was there the day Ray died."

She took a breath and added, "And so was Mad Dog."

Twenty

Jill adjusted her position in her chair so she could speak quietly. I leaned closer, knowing this was the final door in her heart to open.

"Ray was a location manager. He would go ahead of the production company and scout out locations for a shoot, but…I'm sorry—you know what a location manager is."

"That's okay. Just say whatever you want to say."

"I got so used to telling the story for the reporters and the lawyers. Let me start again." She took a tiny sip of her cappuccino to fuel her efforts.

"Ray had scouted a location for a Jackamond coproduction. It was at Oriental Bay, which isn't far from here. The site was an old warehouse on the wharf. Ray obtained all the clearances to use the warehouse, and it passed the safety inspection, so he went down with a small team to run some test shots. The editing department reviewed the shots and made some recommendations for the lighting."

Like Jill, I was familiar with the steps taken before the actual shooting. But I was feeling a lurch in my stomach. I knew about the warehouse accident. And not just because of Tony's job. The trade journals ran articles on it, pointing out the unnecessary risks taken in the increasingly competitive film industry. I didn't stop Jill to tell her that. I wanted her to have the freedom to say whatever she needed to.

"Ray took me with him that day. We planned to go to lunch after the test shots. Mad Dog met us there, and the three of us went into the building. The structure looked reliable; otherwise, we wouldn't have gone in. The rest of the crew hadn't shown up yet."

Jill swallowed. "The authorities think it might have been the strain from the camera crew and all their equipment in the warehouse a few days earlier, but no one knows exactly why the floor broke through. Ray and Mad Dog fell into the water. I was standing back and lost my balance, but I didn't fall in."

She blinked back the tears. "I thought it was going to be like in the movies. They would come bobbing up in the water, laughing like Mel Gibson and Danny Glover."

The first tear rolled over her cheek. "But when I moved closer to the edge, I could see that it was a mess under the wharf. Cement blocks were sticking up, and sharp boards floated on top of the dark water. Ray surfaced with blood on his forehead. He called out my name, and I yelled back that I was okay.

"Then he called out, 'Mad Dog,' and I screamed, 'Ray, don't go back under!' But he did. Mad Dog was unconscious, so Ray pushed him up to the surface and tried to get him balanced on one of the protruding blocks of cement. Then Ray just slipped back down under the water. We found out later he had broken his ankle and several ribs when he fell. One of the broken ribs punctured his right lung and…"

My hand closed around Jill's wrist. I gave her a comforting squeeze. "You don't need to say any more." I knew the story from there. Mad Dog had a broken arm and a concussion. The court case against the studio had become cumbersome because the wharf was part of a historical site, and a former studio employee testified that Mad Dog had a reputation for being reckless.

Reaching into my purse with my free hand, I offered Jill a tissue and kept one for my tears as well.

"You know what?" She dabbed her eyes. "It feels different telling this to you. I've told it so many times to so many people who wanted to pick apart the facts. I feel like I don't have to explain any of it with you. I can just put it out there and let it be what it is."

All kinds of thoughts raced though my mind as I fumbled to find something comforting to say. But I didn't let a single syllable slip from my lips. It was not my place to label this experience for Jill; my part in her life was to be her friend. Sometimes true friends say the most when they don't say anything.

Tracey returned to the table, introduced us to Susanne, and after a few moments of polite conversation, we ended our girls' night out with Tracey single-handedly carrying the conversation all the way home. Fortunately, this wasn't a challenge for dear Tracey.

Tony was waiting up. I told him everything.

"I never made the connection that Jill was Ray's wife," he said.

Tony told me that Mad Dog never had talked about the accident. Tony hadn't put the pieces together.

"I'm having a hard time finding a place to put these feelings. I mean, I like Mad Dog, of course. I'm glad he's still alive. But Ray sounds like he was an amazing man. If God was going to rescue one person from that fall, why did he choose Mad Dog?"

Tony looked stunned.

"What are you thinking?" I asked.

"You used the word *fall*," he said.

"Right. They fell through the floor."

"I know. I've heard the story a dozen times. I just never got it. It's a perfect picture."

Once again my husband had edited his thoughts so quickly I was lost. "A perfect picture of what?"

"Christ. Why did He rescue any of us after the fall? He gave up His life for us."

I didn't like Tony's edited version of the traumatic events one bit. For hours I lay awake rearranging all the information my brain had been given that night. The only settling thought I could manage was that I, too, had been rescued after the fall. It wasn't because of anything I had done, but God's extravagant love had reached down and rescued me, taking me from death to life.

I wanted my life to count for something. I wanted to live out the rest of my days expressing that same extravagant love to others. I didn't want to be cautious and live out a string of unfulfilled days, pitifully folded up into myself. I wanted full days and a full life.

It occurred to me, as dawn softly brought her warming glow through the curtains, that I had just been given the answer to my math equation. Forty-five years plus extravagant love would equal the kind of life I wanted to live, no matter how many days or years were left.

By noon I was done with all the pondering. I wanted to be with Jill. I called and asked if she wanted to meet for a latte.

"Would you mind coming to my house instead? I'm not dressed for going out, but you're welcome to come over."

All the way to Jill's I wondered if the events of last night had sent her into a slump. I expected to find her in her pajamas when she opened the door, but instead, she was wearing tattered painting clothes.

"Come see what I've done."

Jill led me to her bedroom and opened the door to show me the half-finished paint job. All her furniture was covered with plastic tarps; she had taped the edging of the baseboards. The color was a rich shade of pumpkin orange.

"Wow!" I said.

"I've had the paint for a couple of years. Ray and I were always going to do this when we had time, but you know what? We never had time. I have time. I woke up at 4 AM and decided I had time to do this. What do you think of the color?"

"I love it."

"Really?"

"Reminds me of an orange grove," I said with a warm smile.

"That's what I thought, too."

"Do you want some help?"

"You're dressed too nicely," Jill said.

"No, I'm not. Give me an old shirt like you're wearing, and I'll be fine. I don't care about these jeans."

Jill looked at the shirt she had on. It hung off her shoulders and almost to her knees. "This was one of Ray's," she said with the corners of her lips upturned.

"He was a big man!" I wished the words hadn't flipped out of my mouth the way they had.

"Yes, he was," Jill said proudly. "He was an awesome man. A very big man." She tilted her head. "Do you want to see our wedding pictures?"

"What about painting the room?"

"I need a break," she said. "I want you to see our pictures."

For the next two hours, Jill took me to visit her life when Ray ruled the world. She likened it to when dinosaurs ruled the planet, because he was larger than life. I loved hearing the stories and watching her face light up with each page she turned. I was still processing the details of Ray's death, as if it had just happened the night before. Jill was moving forward. She undoubtedly had relived the experience a thousand times. Now she was thinking about other things. She was in such a different place from the person I had met less than two months earlier.

"I've been thinking about what you said about going to Paris," Jill said.

"Paris?"

"Giving the art tours," Jill said.

"You were the one who brought up Paris," I reminded her with a tease in my voice. "Something about art museums and your friends Mona and Monet."

"Mona?"

"Lisa." The way I said it sounded as if I were trying to play a swimming pool game of Marco Polo.

Jill laughed. "I'm considering leading art tours to Paris. So what do you think of that?"

"I think Bob's your uncle, and the world is waiting for all you have to offer."

Jill filled her quiet home with the sweetest, most endearing laughter. "It's more like, God's my Father, and He has a handful of mercies He's been waiting to give me."

On that note, Jill and I turned our attention to her paint job. We came up with all kinds of new decorating ideas, including the upside-down parasol as a light fixture.

"All we have to do now," I said, "is go shopping for a parasol."

"Oh, isn't that too bad; we have to go shopping."

"And get someone from the studio to come over and rewire the light. I'll ask Tony to have one of the lighting guys over."

"Make sure he doesn't ask anyone in special effects. When we first moved in, Ray had a special effects guy wire our front patio for us."

"What happened? I would think he'd do an extremely good job."

"*Extreme* is the key word in that sentence. I had a laser show on my front deck every time I turned on the lights. If we had music going while we were out there, the lights pulsed with the music. The neighbors thought the wacky Americans were trying to host an outdoor disco."

"Is it still hooked up?"

"No, I dismantled the system."

"By yourself?"

"Never underestimate the power of a woman with a pair of wire cutters."

It seemed Jill was about to surpass me as the queen of one-liners the way she was going.

During the next week we shopped till we dropped or one of Jill's hot flashes made us stop. We found the perfect parasol along with an assortment of must-haves such as nightstands, a shower curtain, a waffle maker, and eight CDs with fun music that got Jill's head and shoulders bobbing whenever she put one on.

I told Tony it was like having a baby shower, the way we were buying everything Jill needed to prepare for her new life. She said she was making up for not buying anything other than food the past two years.

Ten days after starting the renovation, Jill's home felt new. She and I had painted three more rooms, hung new curtains, and had one of the living room chairs reupholstered. Her beautiful wooden bowl from the Saturday market in Sydney sat in a prominent place on the coffee table. In the bowl she cradled a handful of postcards from the locales she and I had been.

We were rearranging the furniture when, out of thin air, Jill said, "There's one thing I didn't tell you about Ray, and I think I need to tell you now."

I found it hard to believe there was any detail about Ray I didn't know. While we had been working side by side for the past week and a half, Jill had reminisced about Ray as a sort of final cleansing. With each story from their years together, she seemed to find a place to put that experience in the new structure of her future. I was there mostly to listen and wield a steady paintbrush.

I leaned against the edge of the couch. "What's that?"

"It's actually more about Mad Dog than it is about Ray." Jill brushed the bangs out of her eyes with the back of her wrist. "For the last few weeks, of all the things I've thought through hundreds of times, this is the part that has bothered me the most."

"Do you mean since you saw Mad Dog at the Embassy Theatre?"

Jill nodded. "You saw the look on his face. All that shame and regret is still there. I never told you, but Mad Dog came to my house after the settlements were finalized. I was still so raw inside. I remember opening the door that day, seeing Mad Dog, and feeling like I wanted to hurt him."

"You weren't ready to face him, I'm sure."

Jill seemed to have made so much progress in finding peace. I didn't want her to digress now. Especially for an un-settled feeling she had about Mad Dog.

"It was more than that. I…" She folded herself into the cor-ner easy chair. "I hated him. There, that's the truth; I've said it aloud. Finally. I hated him. Mad Dog lived, and Ray died, and I hated him for that."

I pulled up a chair and sat across from Jill.

"When Mad Dog came to me, he tried to apologize. He said he knew Ray was a good man, and Ray should have been the one who lived and not him. I just stood there. I didn't say anything. I think he was looking to me for a release of some sort." Jill started to cry. I hadn't seen her cry for days.

"And what did you say to him?"

"I told him…" Jill swallowed and cried some more. "I told him I had nothing to say to him. I said he would have to live with what happened the same way I had to live with it."

She wiped her tears on her sleeve. "You know what? I'm embarrassed to admit this, but I was okay with that until the day I met you."

"The day you met me?"

She nodded. "It was something you said. You said that you

were the one who has enjoyed the reward of my husband's zeal because he saved those crazy orange trees."

For an instant I was really worried about Jill. I wasn't tracking with her logic. Maybe she was tipping off-center emotionally because of all the processing she'd been through during the past few weeks.

"When you said that, Kathy, I immediately thought of Mad Dog. I didn't want to think of him, but his face was right there in front of me. And as clear as we're talking now, I thought, 'Mad Dog's life is also the reward of my husband's zeal, and a human life matters more than a couple of trees.'"

I didn't know how to respond.

Jill drew in a deep breath. "At Ray's funeral the pastor read a verse from John in which Jesus said there's no greater love than for a man to lay down his life for his friend. When the pastor read that, everyone looked at Mad Dog, but I couldn't look at him. I still can't look at him. I don't hate him anymore. I feel something different for him, but it's not hate."

I blinked back the tears that had been brimming my eyelids and looked at the postcards fanned out inside the wooden bowl on the coffee table. The card on top was the picture of the Victorian woman from the museum in Sydney. She now stood in the center of Jill's living room, cradled by the bowl and holding a treasure in her hand.

"I don't know what to do," Jill said.

"Open your hand." I didn't know why I said that or what it meant.

"What?"

I tipped my head toward the postcard. "What do you have in your hand?"

Jill looked at her palm. "Nothing. Except a small callus

under my wedding band. That's all. Are you saying it's time for me to remove my wedding band?"

"No. I mean, I don't know. I was looking at the postcard, and that thought just popped into my head. I don't know what it's supposed to mean. I don't know what you're supposed to do."

I felt so foolish. *Why did I say that? Just because I inadvertently said something meaningful without knowing it the day I met Jill doesn't mean I'm a fountain of wisdom. But she's waiting for me to spout the next life-changing one-liner.*

"Jill, how about if we finish moving the furniture around, and then we can talk some more about this."

"I don't have anything else to say. I know it's awkward because Tony works for Mad Dog and you've known him all these years. That's why I kept this to myself for so long."

"I'm glad you got everything you're feeling out in the open. I just don't know what to do with it."

Jill rose, and with a slight shrug, she said, "Neither do I."

Twenty-one

On our final day of touch-ups to complete Jill's renovations, we talked Mr. Barry into bringing Dorothea over to see the changes I'd been telling her about. He pushed her wheelchair up the steps to the deck and into the living room.

From Dorothea's position in the middle of the room at renovation central, she used her pointer finger on her left hand to direct the final-day operations. I saw what Mr. Barry meant about the red nails. Those baby fireballs could grab your attention from all the way across the room. All it took was one wag of her index finger, and I hopped up to move a lamp or a chair a few inches to the right or left to satisfy our sweetest critic. Dorothea was a happy woman that day.

So was Jill.

Mr. Barry took Dorothea home in the late afternoon. We invited them to stay for dinner, but Dorothea had worn herself out giving directions. Tony had agreed to come over to Jill's with the lighting guy since the parasol light was the final detail that needed to be put in place. Jill offered to prepare dinner for the lighting guy in return and opened the invitation to Tony and me as well.

She and I went to work in her newly spruced-up kitchen. Jill had promised me she would make her favorite New Zealand lamb dish with her version of Pavlova if I'd make something American.

A few days earlier, Skyler had sent me a box of Cheerios as a joke. I brought the box with me to Jill's that day, but I hadn't shown it to her. All I said was that I had the first course covered. I also brought all the ingredients to make chocolate chip cookies from a recipe I knew by heart.

The weather was nice enough for us to have dinner on the front deck so, as soon as the cookies were in the oven with the timer set, I volunteered to set the patio table.

"Do you need salad plates?" Jill asked, trying to guess what I'd brought for the first course.

"No, soup bowls. And some milk. And maybe some sugar."

Jill grinned. If she had guessed my surprise, she was being gracious enough not to spoil my fun. Giving me what I needed, she sent me to the deck where I poured the happy treat into the bowls. Then, because no one was watching, I picked up one of the golden rings, held it between my fingers, and murmured, "My precious!"

Then I popped it in my mouth.

I would have performed my tribute at dinner, but I didn't know whom Tony was bringing from the studio with him. If it was a true Middle-earth kind of guy, I might be putting Tony's job in jeopardy. And that would not be good, since Tony still hadn't heard if he'd gotten the position on the next project.

I lit all the candles in the whimsical holder that circled the center of the patio table. That's when I noticed the wire that led up the center of the umbrella pole and spread out along the spokes with hundreds of twinkle lights.

Ten minutes later, I opened the front door. "Jill, can you come out here a minute?"

Jill arrived, drying her hands with a dishtowel. I plugged in a cord, and the twinkle lights inside the umbrella lit up—along with the blue and green laserlike light show.

"What did you do?"

I held up my two tools. "Never underestimate the power of a woman with a pair of wire cutters *and* a roll of duct tape!"

The studio van stopped at the bottom of the driveway.

"Good. The lighting guy and Tony should be able to fix this." Jill reached over to pull the plug before it started an electrical fire.

Lifting my head, I saw Tony coming up the driveway. Next to him was Mad Dog.

"Tony!"

Of all the people you could have chosen, why did you choose Mad Dog?

"It's okay." Jill stopped me before I pulled out a one-liner that I wouldn't be able to swallow later. "I asked Tony to bring him."

"You did?"

"Yes."

Jill looked calm, but I felt rattled. Mad Dog was the last person I thought she would ever want to see. Especially in her own home.

Mad Dog came up the steps and walked toward us on the deck. At first his head was down, but as he came closer, he cautiously glanced up at Jill. She met his gaze, and the two of them looked at each other. Not the way they had awkwardly glanced back and forth at the Embassy Theatre. This time they met each other eye to eye.

Jill took two steps toward Mad Dog. "The last time you stood here at my door, I told you I had nothing to say to you. I do have something to say to you now."

She lifted her chin and held out her open palms, as if offering the invisible treasure Mad Dog had once come seeking. Her voice was a whisper. "It's okay, Marcus. Really. I don't hold anything against you. Not anymore. I want you to have your life back. All of it."

Apparently while Jill and I had been renovating her home, God had been doing some renovating inside the home of her heart. Tonight was open house.

Mad Dog just nodded, but I saw a light in his eyes that I hadn't realized had gone out until it came back on.

With few words, the four of sat down to our bowls of Cheerios. I looked out at the sea and watched as the Southern Cross began to traverse the evening sky. God was filling His treasure chest with extravagant mercies; somewhere, on the other side of this planet, it was a new day.

Epilogue

Tony didn't get the position at Jackamond Studios, so we didn't stay for another three months. He actually finished his project ten days ahead of schedule. It was his gift to me, he said, so we could see more of Australia and New Zealand together before we had to fly back to California.

At first I took it hard that he didn't get the job extension. I had come to love New Zealand so much that I didn't want to leave. I told Tony that, and he asked me, "What do you love about New Zealand?"

I only had to think for a moment before I gave him the answer. "It's the people, it's the people, it's the people."

Dorothea cried when I kissed her good-bye. Her great big, blobby tears and all those deep-throated guttural sounds didn't scare me one bit when she tried to communicate. I told her I was going home so I could attend school to learn how to become a speech therapist for stroke victims. That's when Mr. Barry got blinky-eyed, too.

Tracey filled every empty corner of my packed luggage with bags of chocolate fish. "For all the times you need to reward yourself for doing a little sumthin' good," she said.

Mad Dog is back here in Los Angeles. He and Tony have worked together on two projects since their New Zealand days. Their most recent project won an Oscar. It wasn't the first Oscar won by a film Mad Dog worked on. But it was the first one he had worked on since he had become an unshakable God-follower.

In a concise manner, Tony said Mad Dog trusted Christ the night we stood on Jill's front deck. My husband had gotten into a complicated discussion with Mad Dog earlier that week at the studio about why God's Son had to come in after us because of our fall into sin. Mad Dog and Tony held opposite views until that moment when Jill stepped forward and gave Mad Dog the treasure she held in her hand. Then Mad Dog understood about extravagant sacrifices and the love attached to them.

Jill and I decided a week before Tony and I left that we didn't believe in saying good-bye to each other. She suggested we say *au revoir* instead. That's because she was listening to a French language program and ordering French movies to watch. We both knew that Paris would become a reality for her.

"And depending on which way around the globe this little free bird flies," Jill said, "I would estimate that a certain house next to two old orange trees is exactly halfway between here and Paris."

That was three years ago. Jill has been to Tustin to see me five times already. She's been to Paris three times and has two more grandbabies.

Her most recent visit was last month, and I think that's

what prompted me to write down our story. That and the fact that to celebrate Jill's visit, Tony strung a big hammock for us between the orange trees. "Ray's orange trees" we now call them.

Jill and I tottered out to the hammock the night she arrived, armed with a mound of comforters. We got ourselves balanced—a very important aspect of any form of art, including verbal scrapbooking. There, beneath a canopy of orange blossoms, we cut and pasted our favorite shared memories such as sipping mocha lattes at the Chocolate Fish, painting Jill's walls and Dorothea's red fingernails, the fallen lawn hobbit, the above-water ballet troupe, feeding the kangaroos, the lights on Sydney Harbor, and Evan the singing punter.

Then, because I'd waited a long time to do this, I sat up straight and said, "Jill, don't move! There's a lizard—"

I didn't have a chance to finish my joke before Jill turned the prank on me. In one motion the two of us were tumbled down under once more. This time it was only down under the emptied hammock, where we landed together on soft California orange grove soil.

We laughed until the neighbor's dog started to bark. Then, with all the comforters tucked around us, we settled into the best years of our friendship like two sassy mama birds swaying back and forth in a big, fluffy nest. We were at home with each other. No matter what side of the globe we were on. We both knew it would be that way the rest of our lives. And forever.

Discussion Questions

1. When she arrives in New Zealand, Kathleen finds herself without a close circle of friends for the first time in her life. Have you ever found yourself in a season of life without a single close girlfriend to share the journey with you? Did you go looking for one, or did one find you?

2. Why do you think Kathleen never took on the nickname "Kathy" before? Do you think she went back to "Kathleen" when she returned to California? Have you ever had a nickname that marked a significant change in your life?

3. Do you think Kathy would have agreed to drive a vintage truck in California, or did she jump at the chance just because she was in New Zealand? Have you ever found it easier to try a new experience when you're in a brand-new place?

4. Did Kathy seem like the kind of woman who was given to extreme mood swings the way Tony observed after she knocked over the hobbit? Or were the emotional dips and highs all part of the adjustments she had to make in order to find her place in Wellington?

5. Have you ever felt like you were eighteen again? What experience prompted that feeling?

6. Why was it hard for Jill to talk about Ray with Kathy? Do you think Kathy did the right thing to simply listen, or should she have asked more questions about Ray earlier?

7. What did you observe about the ways Jill processed her grief? Have you experienced grief in your life? If so, how did you process it?

8. How do you feel when you are around people like Dorothea? Have you ever known someone like Mr. Barry?

9. Why do you think it was important for Jill and Kathy to get away and have a little adventure in Christchurch? How did that experience bond their friendship? How have adventures bonded some of your friendships?

10. Have you ever been amazed by an animal the way Kathy was enraptured by the kangaroo? What was it, and how did it affect you?

11. How would you have answered the question Jill asked Kathy: "Do you think God is fair?"

12. What did Jill mean when she told Mad Dog she wanted him to have all of his life back?

13. How did Jill and Kathy both receive and express "extravagant love"? How do you see that kind of extravagant love showing up in your life?

14. When they see the painting of the Victorian woman on the shore, Jill tells Kathy that she holds a treasure in her hand, although she doesn't yet know what it is. It later turns out to be forgiveness for Mad Dog. What unrecognized treasure do you hold in your hand?

More Sisterchick Adventures
by
ROBIN JONES GUNN

SISTERCHICK n.: a friend who shares the deepest wonders of your heart, loves you like a sister, and provides a reality check when you're being a brat.

SISTERCHICKS ON THE LOOSE

Zany antics abound when best friends Sharon and Penny take off on a midlife adventure to Finland, returning home with a new view of God and a new zest for life.

1-59052-198-6

SISTERCHICKS DO THE HULA

It'll take more than an unexpected stowaway to keep two middle-aged sisterchicks from reliving their college years with a little Waikiki wackiness—and learning to hula for the first time.

1-59052-226-5

SISTERCHICKS IN SOMBREROS

Two Canadian sisters embark on a journey to claim their inheritance—beachfront property in Mexico—not expecting so many bizarre, wacky problems! But they're nothing a little coconut cake can't cure...

1-59052-229-X

a sisterchicks® novel

THE GLENBROOKE SERIES
by Robin Jones Gunn

Come to Glenbrooke…a quiet place where souls are refreshed.

SECRETS *Glenbrooke Series #1*
Beginning her new life in a small Oregon town, high school English teacher Jessica Morgan tries desperately to hide the details of her past.

1-59052-240-0

WHISPERS *Glenbrooke Series #2*
Teri went to Maui hoping to start a relationship with one special man. But romance becomes much more complicated when she finds herself pursued by three.

1-59052-192-7

ECHOES *Glenbrooke Series #3*
Lauren Phillips "connects" on the Internet with a man known only as "K.C." Is she willing to risk everything…including another broken heart?

1-59052-193-5

SUNSETS *Glenbrooke Series #4*
Alissa loves her new job as a Pasadena travel agent. Will an abrupt meeting with a stranger in an espresso shop leave her feeling that all men are like the one she's been hurt by recently?

1-59052-238-9

CLOUDS *Glenbrooke Series #5*
After Shelly Graham and her old boyfriend cross paths in Germany, both must face the truth about their feelings.

1-59052-230-3

WATERFALLS *Glenbrooke Series #6*
Meri thinks she's finally met the man of her dreams...until she finds out he's movie star Jacob Wilde, promptly puts her foot in her mouth, and ruins everything.

1-59052-231-1

WOODLANDS *Glenbrooke Series #7*
Leah Hudson has the gift of giving, but questions her own motives, and God's purposes, when she meets a man she prays will love her just for herself.

1-59052-237-0

WILDFLOWERS *Glenbrooke Series #8*
Genevieve Ahrens has invested lots of time and money in renovating the Wildflowers Café. Now her heart needs the same attention.

1-59052-239-7